LIFE'S DILEMMA

LEN TITOW

SWEETSPIRE LITERATURE
MANAGEMENT

‘I WILL SCATTER
YOU TO THE FOUR
CORNERS OF THE
EARTH AND BRING
YOU BACK’

CHAPTER 1

Sue Pulsar points a gun in her husband's direction. With blood streaming from her nose and blood shod eyes, she said, 'You are nothing but a bastard. You belt me and the kids up for no reason other than you are mean and cannot control your temper. Well, we will not take it anymore. Collect your things and get out of here, now!'

Her husband turns to walk away but then suddenly rushes at Sue, who, seeing her life in danger, squeezes the trigger of the gun she was holding.

There is a loud bang, and her husband falls face down on the floor, motionless. Blood flowing from his chest.

Sue runs over to him and turns him over and could see she had shot him through the heart. She walks to the phone in a daze and dials 911.

The producer calls out, 'Cut' and the filming stops.

Producer said, 'Thank you all. This ends the filming. As you know, we will do a preliminary editing of the film over the next three days, and you are all asked to take it easy but be available just in case we need to do another shot if a take is not up to our standards. Everyone, have a good rest and enjoy your break. We will be in touch. Otherwise, we will see you all in three days' time.'

Sue heads back to her caravan, which was on site, and on the way got something to eat. Pondering in the caravan, she wonders, what will she do for three days in this shoe box? She stares at the roof of the caravan and decides she needed a break, possibly an exploration of the countryside. She packs some clothes in a bag and gets into her car and drives off to see what the countryside looks like and what can occupy her for three days. It wasn't long before she was heading down one of the main highways.

After travelling for about two hours, Sue developed a dry throat and was getting thirsty. Spotting a roadside cafe up ahead, she drives into the parking area. She gets out and goes inside and looks at the board as to what is available. She orders a hamburger and coke and sits at one of the tables. Shortly thereafter, her order is brought to her table. She eats her meal. Drinks her coke and waits for about fifteen minutes, then decides to move on. After paying her bill, she goes to the bathroom, attends to her toilet needs, and then walks to her car to continue her journey.

As she continues driving for about two more hours, she is alerted to a noise coming from the front of her car and realises that the front wheel is making a noise that resembles driving with a square wheel. It dawns upon her that one of her tyres is flat and she needs to replace it with the spare, which is in the boot.

She passes a large building with a high brick wall around it and drives into the driveway and stops to see if anyone can help her change her tyre.

Sue gets out of her car and goes to the front door and rings the doorbell. No answer, so she rings it again and eventually a nun comes to the door who says, 'Can I help you?'

Sue says, 'I have a flat tyre. I wonder whether you have someone that can help change it for me.'

The nun stares at Sue and says, 'I will ask Nicholas to attend to that for you. Would you like to come on in and wait in our lounge room?'

Sue says, 'Yes, thank you. That is kind of you.'

The nun takes Sue to a large room which has about ten children sitting down on the floor doing some craft with crayons.

Sue says, 'I hope I am not interrupting one of your bibles reading sessions.'

Nun said, 'O no. The children come from the orphanage we run. We take care of about fifty children who either have been abandoned by their parents or have found themselves homeless for whatever reason. By the way, my name is Sister Mary. I am one of the nuns at St Joseph.' She stretches out her hand.

Sue immediately takes her hand and said, 'My name is Sue Pulsar. Thank you for helping me with the flat tyre.'

Sister Mary said, 'I thought I recognised you. You're that film star.'

Sue said, 'Yes, I have done several films. We had just completed a film not far from here, and I thought I would take a couple of days to look around before going back home.'

Sister Mary said, 'Let me show you around and we can get Nicholas to change your tyre.'

At that point, a little boy comes up to Sister Mary and says, 'Mum, toilet.'

Sister Mary says to Sue, 'Please wait a minute while I attend to some urgent toilet training.' With that, she takes the boy to the toilet and leaves Sue momentarily.

Sister Mary comes back within a few minutes with the boy in hand and says to Sue, 'This is Rodney. One of our orphans.'

Sue says, 'Hallow Rodney and gives Rodney a kiss on the check.'

Rodney says, 'Mum, she's nice.'

Sue says, 'Why does he call you Mum? You are surely not his mother. Are you?'

Mary says, 'No, he just seems to trust me and has adopted me as his mother.'

The two get up and start walking down a corridor, followed by Rodney until they stop outside an office. Sister Mary goes in and starts talking to someone there who comes out and introduces himself as Nicholas Middleton. I am one of the ministers here. Can I have your keys so I can get the spare out of the boot? Sue hands Nicholas the keys and he goes off while the two continue walking down the corridor until they stop at the entrance of a very large room.

Sister Mary says, 'This is one of the dormitories which houses ten children. We have five more like it and all are just about full. The room to your right is where we keep the disabled children who have a physical or mental problem and require more attention than the others.'

Sue steps into the disabled dorm and notices two of the children are seated on their beds, not moving around. She says, 'What is wrong with those children?'

Sister Mary says, 'They have had problems at birth, and both need an operation to correct a defect which is preventing them from being mobile and active like a five-year-old should be.'

Sue says, 'Why don't you get them attended to?'

Sister Mary says, 'We do not have the money to do that, nor do we have the doctors who specialize in that type of operation. The problem is that the two children will most probably never get the help they need and if the injury is left too long, then it would not be possible to correct the damage.'

Sue moves up to the two children, who smile as she approaches them. They reach out to give her a hug. She hugs them and puts them back on their beds.'

Sister Mary moves on with Rodney next to her and singles to Sue to catch up to her. They walk along and then enter a large church. They go inside and both sit in one pew upfront with Rodney in between them.

Sister Mary says, 'As you can see, we have a very basic church. Sadly, the bandits have stolen all our golden chalices and icons. They often target places like ours to steal and sell items for money. We have been raided twice this month and one of our ministers was shot dead trying to stop them from taking the golden challises. Thank God they haven't taken the wooden cross, as that is the most precious item in the church.

Sue looks at the wooden cross, which has a red robe slung over the arms of the cross. She stares at it and says, 'It doesn't seem to me to be of any great value.'

Sister Mary says, 'No, it doesn't, but we believe it is the cross on which Jesus Christ was crucified on, and we have found it has performed miracles which adds to the credibility of what we say.'

Sue says, 'How did you come by it?'

Sister Mary says, 'You wouldn't believe me, but many years ago, it was brought to us by a donkey. Coincidently, at that time, the then archdeacon was looking for a cross for the church. One parishioner who was a carpenter put it together, and it has been there ever since. People with medical conditions have prayed at the foot of the cross and have been healed and this has not just happened once, but many times.'

As they were talking, a donkey walks into the church and stops in front of the cross. He pauses for a moment, not moving, then dips his head to the cross and kneels before it and stays in that position for about twenty-second. He then stands up and walks out of the church.

Sue says, 'How often does he do that?'

Sister Mary says, 'Once or twice a day. We look after him in the barn and he has the freedom of the grounds to wander wherever he desires. It is said that his ancestor was the donkey Jesus rode on at Palm Sunday when he entered Jerusalem. This is why he takes a great interest in the Cross. As if he is the keeper.'

Sue says, 'Well, there is no doubt you have a lot going for you with the church and the orphanage.'

Sister Mary says, 'Yes, but it will soon have to end as we are running out of money and the donations are not coming in, as in previous years.'

Sue says, 'How much do you need to carry on for a year?'

Sister Mary says, 'a million dollars.'

Sue says, 'I can well imagine it takes quite a bit of money to keep the orphanage going and to operate the church and help the community.'

As they were talking, Nicholas came in and handed the keys back to Sue, saying the tyre had been changed over and she could now drive back home.

The three plus Rodney stepped outside behind the church and noticed a large black cloud moving towards them. Sister Mary says, 'We are in for a dust storm. You better stay the night and head off the next morning. The storm will stop you from seeing the road and you most likely would end up having an accident.'

Sue says, 'Thank you, but I do not want to put you to any trouble.'

Sister Mary says, 'No trouble at all. You can help feed some of the young children. We will put you up in the spare room.' With that, Sister Mary went off, with Sue and Rodney following behind. After a minute, they entered a large room and Sister Mary says, 'I will loan you one of my pyjamas for the night.'

As they walked back to the main lounge room, they could hear the dust storm move over, covering everything with a fine film of sand. It was not possible to see more than a few feet, as the storm was very dense, swirling around, showing it would last for hours.

Sue, Rodney in hand, and Mary went into the kitchen, where the children's food was being prepared. Sue noticed that the meal was very basic and there was not much food available. She says, 'I see the children are not getting very much to eat.'

Sister Mary says, 'We try to do the best with what we have and at this stage we have little money to buy any luxuries for the children. We do our best and try to ensure nothing is wasted. The shopkeepers in town donate what they can, but that is still short of what we really need.'

Sue says, when I get back to the States, I will try to get some donations for you. I will raise the matter on talkback radio and gather some interest in the orphanage.

Sue followed Mary and that evening she helped feed the children and played with them. She gave the two disabled children and Rodney more of her time before giving them a big hug and kiss and putting them to bed.

The next morning, Sue was woken by a bell being rung. It was five in the morning. She got up and dressed herself and walked down the hall but couldn't see anyone. She went to the church and saw that all were there for a brief service before starting their day. She sat in a pew while prays were being said and waited until the service had ended. Sister Mary came up to her and invited her to help prepare the children's breakfast, which was very basic, cornflakes and half a piece of fruit.

She stayed to help feed the children, concentrating on the two disabled children and Rodney which she befriended. Once fed, the children were dressed and allowed to play in the large yard at the back of the church. The two disabled children could not play and were limited to siting outside watching the other children run around and enjoy themselves. Rodney went to play but kept an eye on Sue.

Sue looked at the disabled children and decided to do something about their care. She had the money and was not tied up in a relationship. She told Sister Mary that she would talk to some doctors when she returned to the States. To avoid a lifetime of wheelchair use, she wanted to explore the possibility of bringing the children to America for medical treatment.

She went up to her room and gathered her purse. She opened it and took out her cheque book and draw a cheque for one hundred thousand US Dollars. She walked downstairs. Sister Mary was waiting for her, with Rodney in hand. Sue gave Mary a hug and thanked her for her help and kissed Rodney with instructions on him to look after mum. Mary smiled.

Sue says, 'It was my pleasure. I would like to make a small donation towards your orphanage. You might be able to feed the children a little better with this donation.' With that, she handed Sister Mary the cheque, gave her a kiss, and both walked to Sue's car, followed by Rodney. She advised Sister Mary she would be in touch and would try to get some donations for the orphanage once she got back to the States. She gave Rodney a hug and a kiss and got in her car and drove off towards the film studios.

Sue glanced into the revision mirror and could see Sister Mary glancing at the cheque in disbelief, with Rodney beside her. One hundred thousand dollars for changing a tyre. The expression on Sister Mary's face and her waving goodbye will always remain with Sue.

After driving for four hours, Sue got back to her caravan and went inside to rest. Shortly afterwards, there was a knock at her door and a few of her friends came in to see what she got up to. They all went to the canteen where most of the crew was hanging out. They each got a cold drink and sat down. All of them were eager to find out who did what over the last few days.

Sue told everyone what she got up to and gave a description of the orphanage and the fact the children did not have enough to eat. She described the plight of the two disabled children and what she intended to do for them. As she was talking, some of the crew took up a donation and passed a hat around. They collected one hundred thousand dollars.

Because of the acute demand to visiting the orphanage, it was decided to take those interested the next day in two buses. The Director, who was still present, could present the donations collected from the staff to Sister Mary personally.

The next morning, two busloads of crew members headed off towards the orphanage, with Sue giving directions. After travelling four hours, they arrived there, and everyone disembarked and headed for the main entrance.

Sister Mary saw that a crowd of people were walking towards the main entrance and walked out to see what they wanted. Sue moved to the front and greeted Sister Mary, who was surprised to see Sue back so soon. Rodney came out of the Monastery and ran beside Sister Mary and then to Sue. She introduced Sister Mary to the Director who advised that he had been told the orphanage could do with some help. Sister Mary said, 'Yes, we can. It has been a lean year for donations, and we are just about at the point of having to close the orphanage for lack of money.'

The director asked Sister Mary could he be shown around? Sister Mary was very happy to act as the tour leader and off they went, with Rodney and everyone following. Rodney was worried by the number of people there, so he grabbed Sues hand and held onto it. They eventually arrived at the children's dormitory, and all were keen to see the children.

After playing with the children, they gathered in the church. The Director told Sister Mary that they raised $120,000 for the orphanage, and he would match the donation to support their ongoing work.

Sister Mary thanked everyone and mentioned that the bank had notified her they were going to take over the premises and sell everything because they had fallen three months behind on their loan payments. They gave them sixty days to find another place to house the children. The bank did not care what would happen to the children, nor the good work the sisters were doing. All they cared about was their money.

Sister Mary expressed gratitude for the donations and support, as it would save the orphanage from being taken away.

The Director was really interested in the buildings and location of the orphanage. He even wanted to shoot a movie there. The landscape lend itself to several possibilities, and he advised Sister Mary of his interest. If they set up and shoot a film there, it would ensure the orphanage would receive the funds to keep going without threat of eviction.

Sue went specifically to see her two disabled friends, who were thrilled to see her as they thought she had left them. She spent time with them and Rodney, then left them with the sister there. She thanked Sister Mary for her hospitality and boarded the bus for the long trip back to the studio.

CHAPTER 2

Sue sat in her unit in New York, looking over the script her agent had sent her for her next movie. It was to be shot in Mexico and would take about four months to complete. She read the first few pages to get an understanding of the story line and the strength of the characters. As she was reading, her mind was continually thinking about the two disabled children back at the orphanage and the help they needed.

With thoughts of the cheeky Rodney, she smiled and surveyed her unit, feeling a sense of loneliness now that she had nothing to occupy herself with. She realised if she took up this new role, she would not see the disabled children or Rodney for at least half a year. She would also not see Sister Mary, who she befriended and found to be something like a sister to her. They continually kept in touch with each other and often had Zoom sessions on their computers. Each would chat for hours, and they became close friends. Rodney was always there, too. He would smile and say, 'hi mum.'

As Sue was deep in thought, she was brought back to reality with her doorbell ringing. She went to the door and noticed it was her agent on the other side. She opens the door, and her agent says, 'Are you ready? We want this to be a good interview.'

Sue realised she had a television interview scheduled with one of the big names in America on a popular show, which would be televised from coast to coast. The interview was to be about her up-and-coming film, which she just had completed. Sue said, 'Yes. Let's get going as I must get to makeup before the show screens.' They both left the unit and went down to the basement. Got in her agent's car and drove off to the studio.

When they arrived, Sue was quickly taken to makeup to enhance her appearance and give her a glamorous, star-like look.

After makeup, she was rushed through to wardrobe and dressed for the occasion. Two minutes to spare and she was called to wait at the entrance of the show. The presenter made a brief introduction and called out her name. Sue entered on the set at the applause of the audience and walked to where the presenter was standing.

They sat down. The presenter first asked her questions about the film and in particular the storyline which Sue was happy to answer. Sue made it sound as if it was a must-to-see film and did her best to promote it. After discussing the plot and where the film was shot, the presenter asks Sue, 'Did you have time to look around to see what the countryside was like?'

Sue replies, 'Yes. I travelled on a main highway and had to ask for help at a monastery to get a tyre changed over. Attached to the monastery was an orphanage with around fifty children who had been abandoned or had lost their parents for various reasons. Some children unfortunately need medical help, which the nuns cannot provide. There is a scarcity of doctors in that part of the world and in particular specialists to attend to the needs of the children. I was hoping to bring two of the children who are four and five years of age back to the States, to see if an orthopaedic surgent could operate on them.'

'The children are wheelchair bound and have a spinal problem. But this costs a lot of money, so I am not sure we can help the kids to get back on their feet. In fact, the last day I was there, the children were fed a cauliflower meal for dinner, which comprised butter and cauliflower blended into a paste. Nothing else, as they had no money to buy the children fresh vegetables.'

'When I returned to the studio, I shared the story of the kids with everyone. The film crew then passed a hat around, which the director generously matched. We used the funds to pay off the mortgage, which was three-month overdue. The bank told the nuns that if they couldn't pay, they would be evicted along with the children and would need to find a new home. So, it was upsetting to hear of the possibility of fifty children being thrown out on the street.'

The presenter says, 'Folkes. Are we going to allow this to happen? If anyone wants to donate, they can do so. The details are on your screen now. As for the disabled children, we at this station will guarantee the funding of their medical expenses and transport to and from the orphanage.'

With that, there was a prolong burst of applause. Sue burst into tears while the cameras were focused on her. As they were talking, donations came in and after half an hour, they had reached five million dollars. Other stations also aired the interview, which got more people interested in helping the sisters and their orphanage. Someone rang in and asked if they could adopt some children, which no one could answer. Other asked could they go there and help to manage repairs or do whatever was needed to be done.

About ten minutes before the show was due to close a medical team from one of the States major children's hospitals rang through to advise that a team of doctors and nurses were prepared to go there and check out the children and bring back those that needed help. When the audience was advised of this, the whole studio burst into applause. The show had to be wound up as it had gone five minutes over its scheduled time.

Newspapers took up the story and reported on the events and the show, which gathered momentum as the day progressed.

When the American President found out about the broadcast, he went on national television to show his support for the Monastery and orphanage. He guaranteed that the donated funds would reach the Monastery and that the children would be looked after. Those suffering would be flown back to America for treatment.

He advised the nation that America would acquire the Monastery, and this would become part of America's foreign aid to that region. The orphanage would be taken care of and protected from the warring tribes. All donations would go towards maintaining the facilities and to build a medical centre there, with doctors attending rotationally.

Something that started off as a small private encounter developed into a project that swept across the nation and caught the imagination of everyone in America.

The President chose one of his generals to supervise the project and ensure the children received smooth access to medical help. He also noted that the area where the Monastery was located was notorious for tribal attacks. These tribes would steal from the occupiers or hold individual to ransom for large sums of money. He ordered that a military force of one hundred men be sent there to ensure the safety of the nurses and doctors who were to be flown over to look after the children. The President did not want any of these people being held hostage or killed while there.

Within a short period, a plane was allocated by the Airforce, and this was loaded up with provisions and transport to take the personnel from the airport to the Monastery.

Sue was invited to join the group, as she was the one who started the momentum and requested the help on behalf of the orphanage. If she went with them, she would have to postpone her next move. She spoke to the producers who agreed to defer filming, to enable her to look after the children.

Sue telephoned Sister Mary, who had already heard what was happening. She explained what was going to take place and advised the date they would arrive with the medicos.

The television station took it upon themselves to handle the money and all the pledges came to one hundred million dollars. A crew from the station would accompany the medical team so they could film the scene. Arrangements were made for a live stream of the Monastery and orphanage back to the States. A recognised broadcaster was selected along with a film crew. There was a plan to show a one-hour documentary on TV to give everyone a glimpse of the Monastery and the children's living conditions.

Once the government gave their clearance, the group left with military personnel to keep everyone safe.

The flight took about six hours, and everyone was glad to step out of the plane and walk around on dry land. They all assembled for customs clearance and once this was completed boarded buses to go to the American Embassy, where arrangements had been made for their stay.

The next morning, after breakfast, they drove to the Monastery in convoy to ensure no one was ambushed. Among the vehicles were three Australian Bushmaster units that were ideal for quick response in case of an ambush.

Sister Mary greeted Sue with a warm embrace, and she was introduced to the other team members. She was kind enough to show everyone around and then took them to the dormitories to see the children.

Sue told Sister Mary that they had raised one hundred million dollars, which would secure the Monastery and orphanage's future. She also mentioned that the American government planned to acquire the Monastery as part of their foreign aid effort.

The medical team got ready and examined every child. They used their mobile unit to take x-rays and conducted pathology exams as needed. They had underestimated the time required, which meant they had to stay a longer period than first thought. The children with issues were treated on-site with medication and received vaccinations for common childhood illnesses. Those who had more serious problems were marked to return to America for surgery. A total of fifteen children were noted to need surgery, and it was decided that they would be flown back with the returning party.

Some of the army personnel undertook some repair work of the buildings and plumbing, as these skills were not readily available in the region. During the period there were several skirmishes with local tribes, but none were serious, requiring an all-out defence or air force help. They were handled by the ground troops who accompanied the party.

Sue and Mary were inseparable, and both found pleasure in each other's company. They each got to know the other better and agreed to keep in touch. Sue, who was an atheist, tried to get Mary to see there was no real God, whereas Mary tried to get Sue to seek forgiveness of her sins and believe in the true God. This was always a conflict between them. They each disclosed their childhood to the other. Mary coming from a religious family and her father was a priest. Her mother died when she was in her mid-teens and she was left at the Monastery, where she later became a nun.

Sue stayed with her parents until she was eight years of age, when both died in a motor vehicle accident. Sue was placed in foster care and moved between families until she was sixteen. Eventually, she ended up with a family where the father worked with sheet metal and the mother worked in a shop. She was closer to her foster father than her mother as he seemed more approachable and not at arms' length, as was her foster mother. When she finished school, she got a job in a large department store selling dresses in the women's section. One day, she was spotted by a film producer and offered a small part in some films, which then led to larger and better parts over time as she gained experience.

Her foster parents left their total estate to Sue, which allowed her to put down a deposit on a unit in New York, which she still owned and called home.

When Sue was at the monastery, she was always with the two disabled children and Rodney and got to know them better. She was told by one nun that the disabled children's house was bombed by one of the warring tribes who killed their parents and injuring them. Rodney's parents were shot when tribesman attacked their farm looking for cattle or sheep. Rodney escaped, and was found by a passing motorist, wondering along the road barely able to talk, bleeding from a chest wound and dehydrated.

After staying a week, the medical team decided to return to America, as most of their work had been completed and they were running short of medical supplies. They agreed to leave all their dry foods at the Monastery.

The money raised would help the nuns provide more food for the children and build a medical centre for them and the surrounding suburbs. It was agreed that when the children were returned, a group from the engineering corps would accompany them and they would build the hospital along with an operating theatre and consulting rooms. The hospital would be prefabricated. Built in America, transported and assembled on site.

On the last evening, all assembled in the main hall for a few speeches and to give thanks and to say their last farewell. Most of the children had been put to bed and everyone wanted to get a good night's sleep before getting on the plane for the long journey home. It was agreed the children would not be placed on board until all was packed away. All the equipment that was not needed in the future was to be returned to the States, and this was packed away securely in one of the larger cargo planes.

As the chief medical officer was making his last speech, a rocket exploded close to the hall, shattering the glass windows and taking out one side of the building. The peace of the night was interrupted by gunshots and men shouting. The military positioned themselves to defend the Monastery, but they were caught off guard and had trouble determining the direction and size of the attacking force.

A grenade exploded inside the hall and tribesmen tried to enter with guns blazed, shooting anyone in sight. Some nuns were gunned down as they tried to run to safety as were American medical staff who were trying to escape. The military opened fire and repealed the force. Those tribal members that entered the building were shot where they stood as the military fired rockets in the direction the force came from, hitting several trucks, causing them to explode and light up the night.

The military could see that there were approximately thirty men at the outer perimeter who were ready to storm the Monastery, so they aimed at them, thinking that if they were hit, the rest would move back. Sure enough, as soon as the rockets exploded around them, the rest retreated to regroup, and possibly make a further attempt.

After about ten minutes, all seemed to ease off and it could be seen that the tribal force sustained heavy casualties, as they did not expect the military to be there.

One by one, those who crouched down stood up to see what damage had been inflicted. Some Sisters, who were face down, didn't move. Sue ran up to them and turned them over to see if they had sustained an injury from the bomb blast. As she turned them over, she could see that they were dead and could not have avoided their injury. She then moved to Mary. Rodney came into the room and, seeing Mary lying face down, ran up to her yelling 'Mum, mum.' Sue turned Mary over and noticed she had been shot through the heart. She would have been killed instantly, and blood was still seeping from her body.

Sue grabbed Mary's body and yells out, 'God no, not Mary' and burst into uncontrollable hysterics while she hugged Mary's body and kissing her. Rodney froze and stood there, seeing Sue crying hysterically as he had done when his parents were shot in front of him. Some of the medical staff moved to where Sue was and tried to get her to release her grip on Mary. She wouldn't and continued crying over Mary's body. They eventually got her to loosen her grip, and they took Mary's body into another room, along with the three nuns who were killed. One of the other sisters took Rodney away, as he was very stressed to see Mary lying there and not moving and Sue crying over her.

They washed the blood from Sue's hands and arms and took her to her room to change her blood-soaked clothes. She was in a world of her own, not being able to understand what was being said to her, concentrating on Mary.

The military moved out and noted that most of the tribal force had been killed and their transport had been destroyed by rockets. They positioned men at the outer perimeter, just in case a further attempt was going to be made that night.

Sue found it hard to come to terms with what had happened. Her newfound friend, no, her adopted sister, killed in a moment, a wink of an eye. This, to her, proved there was no God. If there was, he would not have allowed Sister Mary to be killed. A saint looking after children in the wilderness. Despite her belief in God, this is what He allowed to happen to Mary at the hands of tribesmen, who were more like animals than men?

She found it hard to sleep that night and was glad when morning came. She went to the kitchen and helped the sisters prepare breakfast for the children and assisted them in feeding them. Anything to get her mind off Mary. Rodney came in and stood near Sue. He would follow her wherever she went, now that she was the only one left, that he knew as mum.

Sue prepared those children who were to be transported back to the States and helped put them on the bus so they could be driven to the airport. When the bus arrived, she helped load the children on board and accompanied them to the airport. Once there, she supervised their loading up into the plane and strapped them in for their flight.

Back in her room, at the Monastery, Sue did not know what to do and pondered on her dilemma. Whether she should stay and help the nuns or go to the States and help with the care of the children. After deciding one way, then changing her mind again and again, she decided to go back to the States and packed a bag in preparation. When the time came, she said her farewells to the nuns that were left behind in tears, as all felt she should have stayed. She assured Rodney she would come back soon.

Rodney, who had lost his parents, and Mary couldn't understand why Sue was leaving him as he now considered her his mum. He wanted to stay with Sue, and it took quite some time to calm him down and reassure him that Sue will come back after she takes care of the other children that were to be operated on.

The American forces withdrew the men after a month as it seems the tribes got the message not to attach the American Monastery. To keep the children and nuns safe, they stationed fifty men at the Monastery, expecting only minor conflicts and not a major assault to occur.

CHAPTER 3

The plane landed safely, and the children were moved to a ward in the hospital. Plans were made to have them operated on in a week's time. Before their operations, they would have a thorough medical exam to assess the seriousness of their injuries from explosions or bullets fracturing their bones. This will include X-rays or CT scans to determine the severity of their injuries.

Doctors were appointed to each of the children and they, after examining the X-rays or CT scans, would nominate the day and type of operation the child required. Some children unfortunately required two or three operations, which had to be scheduled days apart.

The day came when one child Sue befriended was to be operated on. It was a spinal cord operation and if things didn't go right, could cause the child being paralysed for life.

Sue waited in the waiting room and, after three hours, was getting worried. She walked up and down the room and even got herself a cup of hospital coffee, which showed how concern she was.

The surgeon operated for over six hours and informed Sue that the operation took longer than expected because of additional damage that wasn't shown on the scans. They had to fix the damage to the spinal cord in several places.

Sue was allowed to see Timothy, who was still in postoperative care and still asleep. She stayed for about five minutes, then left and went back to her unit.

Sue got herself something to eat and sat down in front of the television to see what had happened in the world while she was at the hospital. She had just finished eating when a news alert was announced that more US troops were being sent to help fight rebels at the newly acquired monastery. The monastery's renovation and expansion, which included a medical centre and operating rooms, caught the interest of local tribal leaders.

Sue thought, what was she going to do with her life? Was she going to continue acting or try to help the Monastery by taking Sister Mary's place, as Mary had asked her to do? Mary often said she was marked to take over the Monastery, but Sue dismissed this as wishful thinking. No doubt it was now a bigger place with more facilities and needed a more disciplined mind to manage, but she was a film star, not a desk jockey. Also, what was going to happen to the two disabled children once they had been operated on? These were the question that were now playing on Sue's mind. She decided not to make her mind up yet, but to wait for the outcome of the operations. She packed everything up and went to bed.

At about three o'clock, she woke up with fright. She had a dream where Sister Mary appeared before her and asked her to take over as the administrator of the Monastery and join the order. The dream begun by Mary saying, 'Sister, do not fret about me, for I am in a better place now.'

Sue couldn't step into Mary's shoes because she didn't share the same religious beliefs that Mary had and questioned why God would let Mary be killed by a tribesman.

The more she thought about it, the more she thought it would not work out and dismissed the idea. She went back to sleep and woke up about seven in the morning. She had her shower, a light breakfast and drove off to the children's hospital to see how Timothy was doing.

As she walked into his ward, she was surprised to see Timothy standing holding onto his bed trying to take steps. His muscles were not developed enough to allow him to move his legs but given a few months of physiotherapy he should be able to manage this.

She walked up to him and gave him a big hug and kiss and lifted him up so he could sit on the bed. She noticed he had some toys in his bed and played with them to get his attention. A doctor came up to her and advised that Timothy should make a full recovery and would get all his mobility back over time. She played with Timothy for about an hour and then went off to see how Sarah was coping.

As she walked into her room, Sarah lit up with a big smile and stretched out her arms. She picked her up and gave her a big kiss and hug and sat her up in bed, talking to her. She stayed for about an hour as Sarah had to have some more scans taken as she was being operated on the next day. She promised to come back soon and with that, left Sarah and went to where Timothy was located. She asked the nurse if she could take Timothy to see his sister and, with her permission, put Timothy in a wheelchair and off they went to see Sarah.

When she wheeled Timothy into Sarah's room, she lit up and screeched with joy at seeing Timothy. Sue pulled the wheelchair alongside of the bed and allowed Timothy to get up. Sarah couldn't believe it. Seeing Timothy standing by himself. After ten minutes, Sue picked Timothy up and put him on Sarah's bed so they could touch each other and play with the toys Timothy had brought with him. After an hour, Sue had to put Timothy back in his wheelchair and with Sarah crying and getting hysterical, pushed Timothy back to his own bed. The nurses calmed Sarah down and promised she would see her brother soon.

Timothy was put back into his own bed but got out and stood, trying to walk. Sue gave him a kiss and while he was occupied, left to go home.

The next morning, she repeated what had transpired with Timothy and began the long wait to see if Sarah's operation was going to be a success. The operation took just as long as Timothy's did and the doctors were hopeful Sarah would come out better than Timothy. Sue went and visited Timothy and stayed with him for two hours and then went back to her hotel.

Sue ordered a small meal and got a phone call from the orphanage about a couple from America wanting to adopt Rodney. The man was a junior minister from the Westcoast of America, and they seem a delightful couple. Sue's immediate reaction was no, Rodney now considers Sue as his mother, now that Mary had gone. She asked for the decision to be delayed so she could talk to Rodney before he left.

The next day she visited Sarah, but she was not standing but lying in her bed, not moving. As she approached her bed, a nurse caught up with her and advised her that the operation did not go well, and the doctors were waiting for scans to see what had gone wrong.

Sue went up to Sarah's bed and leaned over and gave her a big kiss. Sarah tried but couldn't move. She was worse than before the operation. She felt nothing below her chest, which showed a central nerve had been damaged. A permanent disability.

Sue fought back her emotions and went out of the room just as she burst into tears, muttering, where is God. First Mary and now Sarah. To allow this to happen to a young child proved to Sue that there is no God. To allow an innocent child to be permanently paralysed is a clear sign he doesn't exist or doesn't care.

A nurse came up to Sue and gave her some tissues. She stayed in the corridor until she thought she could go back in without becoming emotional. She stayed with Sarah for another hour, then left for the hotel.

Sue sat there for an hour, thinking about what she should do about the children and Rodney. She finally decided it would be best for Rodney to be adopted by the young couple rather than for her messing up his life. She phoned the Monastery and asked the sister to but Rodney on Zoom.

As the session progressed, she told Rodney that Sarah had a large operation, and that she was in America looking after Sarah. She told Rodney that friends of hers were going to take him to their home and he would be looked after by them until she could come back to see him. He wanted to know for how long he would be away before she came to collect him. Sue told him it would be awhile and for him to be a good boy and do as he was asked to do. She didn't want to tell him she would never ever see him again, as this would upset him. He left the Zoom session crying, as he wanted his mother Sue to come back and be with him.

CHAPTER 4

Rodney's new parents were informed of what had happened with him and that he thought Sue would come and collect him later. They were encouraged to get him involved with other children so he would forget Sue over time.

James Mc Dillon was a minister at the local church and his wife, Gretter, longed to have a family. The plan was to adopt another child, possibly a girl some eighteen months after Rodney had settled down.

They sat quietly, listening to what the adoption clerk was saying to them. They read all the adoption papers and acknowledged they understood the requirements. Once they signed the adoption papers, they were taken to another room where Rodney would be brought in, and they could get to know him better.

They sat in the room, which had some toys piled up in a corner just in case they had to break the ice. Rodney came in with the adoption clerk and immediately recognised them as the couple that came to the Monastery to see him a week ago.

They had some presents for him which he was keen to open and play with. After about an hour, they left with Rodney in hand and walked out of the building and headed for the airport. When they landed in America, they caught a bus home as they were only a few suburbs from the airport.

Rodney was shown his room but was scared to sleep in it alone, so they had to lie with him until he fell asleep. He was used to being in an orphanage with ten other children and not on his own. Over time, he would get used to the room and not fear being alone. The room had a lot of toys stacked in it for Rodney to play with.

Friends of the Mc Dillons would bring their children to play with Rodney, so he could get used to his new surroundings and not feel lonely without the Monastery.

After a few months, Rodney settled down and was glad to go to school and meet his new friends. James was pleased with how Rodney adapted, so he decided to change Rodney's name to James Rodney Mc Dillon on the adoption papers. Rodney learned that his father's name was James's senior, so he became known as James junior or jnr. His middle name would now be Rodney. Rodney thought that was great, to be like his father, and told everyone that his name was James jnr. Over time, he dropped using Rodney and was always referred to as James jnr.

Whenever possible, James jnr. would go to church with his father and learned how to handle weddings, christenings, and funerals. As his father got older, James jnr. would take over more and more of the work his father normally handled.

After finishing high school, James was able to enter seminary and after a few years, became an ordained minister. His father was pleased with his son and leaned on him a lot for help, especially after his wife died from cancer.

CHAPTER 5

The American Government wanted to fulfill their promise of building a medical facility at the monastery to support the community and orphanage. None existed in the area, which necessitated travelling for hours if you needed basic medical treatment.

Engineers were dispatched to the region along with architects to design the medical facilities. The army would protect these personnel while they went through the design and construction phase.

Plans were drawn up and the procurement orders issued for the prefabrication of the buildings. Orders were sent out for the procurement of medical equipment, which sometimes took months to build.

The design included three medium-sized wards, two operating theatres, two contamination rooms, four consulting rooms connected to a main reception area, and an X-ray unit with a separate CAT scan unit. The joke of the day was whether a domestic cat would do rather than a feral cat for the CAT scans.

Doctors Without Borders would initially supply the doctors on a rotation basis. There were also to be two robotic theatres where operations could be performed robotically anywhere in the world. Finally, new quarters were needed to house the medical staff who would be needed to run the clinics.

The buildings, dormitories and medical facilities were to be away from open spaces as the tribes may destroy the facilities during one of their raids. It was agreed that the facilities would be two stories high, with one storey above ground level. The lower level was to be locked off from the upper level should the raids become uncontrollable.

Once the order was manufactured and received in flatpack, they were loaded onto a wide body plan and freighted to the nearest airport. They were then lifted on site by helicopters. Engineers would accompany the shipment along with tradesmen to erect the buildings.

A continual stream of aircraft was used to ship off the building materials and personnel. It was estimated the construction phase would take about six months and the fit out and testing of equipment a further six months.

Medical equipment which arrived before needed was held in a hanger, awaiting the completion of the buildings.

The initial requirement was the laying of the slab and the sub level plumbing. Specialists were brought in to insure they got this right, otherwise it would be a costly exercise if they had to take up all that concrete and start over again. Care was taken to peg out the sight carefully, and engineers checked the measurements to ensure that the slab was right.

Finally, the day came to pour the footings and slab, which had to be done at the same time because of its size.

After a few days, the slab was poured and left to cure for three weeks. To build on it before it settled and cured would cause the slab to weekend and it could crack.

After the curing period, the builders moved in and erected the framework and roof, which was all cut to requirements.

The bricklayers started laying the bricks, but it took a long time because of production issues with the supply of bricks from the States.

To secure them from lifting during dust storms; the steel corrugated sheeting that comprised the roof had to be screwed down rather than being nailed.

Next, the electrical and plumbing installation took place, which involved piping in oxygen and other gases for medical procedures. Many arguments arose because people disagreed on where to store the gas supply and how to prevent the wrong gas from being supplied. Also, the gas had to be in a relatively secure area to ensure the tanks were not hit if the centre was raided.

After many months, the structure stood completed and the fit-out of all the operating theatres and wards begun. This took over six months, as it was necessary to move connections and re-secure them elsewhere to make things more practical.

It took some two years to complete the building of the facilities and have it to an operational level.

The opening ceremony was a galla affair with many dignitaries coming from the States to look over the facilities.

TV cameras were everywhere capturing the opening, speeches, and showing everything to the contributors in the States.

The military knew that the tribes might attack the centre and harm or capture the dignitaries for ransom.

Extra manpower was brought in to ensure this didn't happen and the extra men stayed a further month after the opening to ensure there was no delayed attack after the facility was opened.

CHAPTER 6

Sue sat in her lounge room, staring at her manager. He was there to set definite dates for the shooting of her next move. He was trying to get Sue to sign the contracts and was having difficulty understanding why she was resisting. The package negotiated was a very lucrative one, which gave her more money than what she had received in other movies. The location was protected and secure and all the main characters were provided with accommodation and a private assistant to take care of the cleaning chores and anything else they may need to handle while they were on the set.

Sue asks her manager to come back the next day as she was in no mood to consider the matter before her. She was upset with what happen to Sarah and couldn't get the two children out of her mind. She was concerned as to what was going to happen to them if she stopped seeing them. Flying back to see how they were going was out of the question. Nor could she take them with her, as she was not their parent or guardian. She just did not know what to do.

After thinking about Sarah, she decided the only thing she could do was to leave her some money, which would allow her to get some things she may need as she grew older. God had abandoned her, leaving her in a worst situation than what she was in before the operation. She could not look after herself and would rely on carers for the rest of her life. While Tim could have a life, but he most probably would stay to look after Sarah.

Sue, being an actress and not a nanny, decided not to get emotionally attached to the children. She preferred to prioritize her own well-being and avoid unnecessary responsibilities.

Sue decided to put the children out of her life and to concentrate on her movie career. She would sign the contract tomorrow and fly to Italy, where the film was being produced. In her opinion, God (if he existed) abandoned Sarah, not Sue, so why should she worry about what would happen to her and Tim. They weren't her children, and she didn't need the responsibility of caring for them, even though she loved them.

Rodney had been adopted by parents in the States and, on all indications, he was finally settling down enjoying family life and playing with his friends. Timothy no doubt would also be adopted out, but it was doubtful anyone would take Sarah.

Sue went to her kitchen and prepared herself a meal and sat in front of the television eating it with a glass of wine. She switched the television on and immediately the news stated two children had been abducted from their home in one of the States in America and police were fearful of the outcome. Sue immediately thought I wonder whether the two could be Tim and Sarah. She realised that the two children were in the States, Boston and not in the Monastery. She switched channels to see if there was a movie on and sure enough, there was, and it was about a family on a holiday. As the movie progressed, the children were being subjected to witnessing several frightful acts which again made Sue think of Tim and Sarah and the life they would have as they grew up.

Sue knew she would have to forget about the children, but this would be easy to think but hard to do.

Immersing herself in a life of make believe was something she knew she had to do, as it was the life of an actor. If reality appeared, this would have to be suppressed with fiction. Her mind kept thinking about the children and wondering how they were and who would look after them, especially Sarah. She knew she cared about them and found this feeling hard to ignore.

Sue didn't believe in God and what had happened to Sarah proved he did not protect or looked after those who believed in him. She switched television channels and came across a gardening program advising how to prepare a bed for planting flowers. Good, this is not about children she thought. As she was looking at the screen, two children appeared and began helping the gardener to mix his soil. Sue again thought of Tim and Sarah and decide to switch the television off and wash her plate ready for the next day. She sat down in the lounge room and picked up a book and began reading it. It was a thriller and Sue thought "No children in this one". As she continued reading, she stumbled upon a plot to kidnap two children and hold them for ransom. She put the book down and decided to have an early night.

As she fell into a deep sleep, she started dreaming about Tim and Sarah and what would happen to them without her guidance and encouragement. She woke up and tried to get them off her mind. She knew she had to do this, otherwise she could not get on with her film career.

Sue got out of bed and sat down in the dark, and wondered what would happen to the children if she was not there. It is all right to say it is not my problem, but you cannot live your life passing on problems that life throws up at you. She stared in the dark and a light flick on and Sue saw Mary standing inches away from her.

Sue froze, not believing what she was looking at. She couldn't utter a word as fear had gripped her.

Mary said, 'You have not learned what is important in life or the value of life. It's clear that your thoughts are only about yourself. You still doubt the existence of Jesus Christ. The children will not be raised by you. You shall not have them. None will be raised by you.'

Sue tried to make out what Mary had said and realised there was no one in front of her, just darkness. After thinking about it, she put it down to her overactive mind and went back to bed, hoping to get some sleep.

CHAPTER 7

The actor that was billed as the main character in the movie was Rick Rodregus. A colourful man that enjoyed the best things that life could offer. He was single. However, it was rumoured that he got a girl pregnant while filming one of his blockbusters, but always denied this. He always thought himself to be a ladies' man and was always with beautiful women. Being non-religious, he gave no thought to God. He had everything he ever wanted, so why worry about God? That was his attitude. He took the view God couldn't provide him with anything better than what he had.

Rick did not consider eternal life was a benefit worthy of giving up what he already had. His focus was on living for today, with no concern for tomorrow.

He was a youngish man who inherited money from his parents, who put him through drama school to allow him to become the film star that he was.

He was known worldwide and featured in several top movies that earned a lot of money. The most fashionable cars were often provided to him by the manufacturer for maximum publicity. He was always seen outside the top clubs with many women adoring the luxuries he provided.

He was no fool in that he refused to touch drugs, nor was he into gambling. At an early age, he discovered he wasn't a drinker and rarely consumed alcohol, even when he was upset. He would sip a glass or two but never empty a bottle.

When in Italy filming, he met a girl who he befriended and took quite a liking to her. He would be seen often with her, and the papers were asking when was the wedding taking place.

He didn't ask about the girl's background as his approach was to love them and leave them. And he intended to leave this girl soon as his next feature film started.

One night when the two were together, the girl told him she was pregnant. He went into a rage and threw her out of his unit, telling her never to come back or tell that lie to anyone else or that he was the father of her child.

The girl called her parents, and they sent a car to pick her up. It so happened that the girl was the daughter of one of the head honchos who associated with the Italian Mafia. Tony Basilischi was her father, and he demanded to hear what had happened.

The girl advised her parents that she was thrown out of his unit when she told him she was pregnant and that he would deny being the father. Tony Basilischi made a phone call and within an hour Rodregus was in his living room. His daughter was sitting in a lounge near to him. Mrs Basilischi was present and sat with her daughter.

Mr Basilischi said, 'My daughter tells me you have been playing around with her while I have been in America. You have got her pregnant and we expect you to do the right thing and marry her. She will have your child, and we will offer you protection as part of the family.

Rodregus says, 'Protection from what, women?'

Mr Basilischi says, 'From death. As a film star, you are just as famous as your next movie. Who do you think funds these movies and ensures they are screened by the major entertainment centres? We tell them what they must show and if you co-operate with us, we will make sure all your movies get priority. Otherwise, you will end up just being a name. No one will want you as a star and you will end up being just a memory.

Rodregus says, 'I don't believe you and I won't marry your daughter. She can have an abortion like all the other girls I have had over the years.'

With that, Rodregus stood up and said, 'Since you brought me here, you can take me back to my hotel.'

Mr Basilischi signalled one of his men standing nearby to do as he has requested. Both men then walked out of the room and Rodregus was taken back to his hotel.

The next day, Mr. Rodregus called his agent to ask about his next film, only to be told that the studio had changed their mind and cast another actor instead of him. He was to finish his current movie and take a holiday. A very long one.

CHAPTER 8

Sue was on site, ready to do her part. As she entered, she could see other actors were rehearsing their lines or ready to move in front of the cameras. She waited until the director gave the order for her to come on site so the next scene could be filmed.

The Director yells out, 'Cut, we'll go with the last scene shot.' Those acting left the scene and those ready to film the next scene entered on the stage. The Director gave an outline of what he was expecting of those actors who were ready to shoot their scene. The scene was set, and everyone went through their lines as a rehearsal.

This routine went on for a further month; they were midway through the movie. Everyone was happy as they were ahead of schedule. For Sue, she had approximately twenty more scenes to shoot with the leading actor Rick Rodregus and was then finished. She had been offered a position in another film, which was to shoot a month after this film was scheduled to end. The only problem was that it would require her to go to Portugal, as that was where the film was being shot in one of the country's many cathedrals. It was a good part, and Sue was thrilled to get nominated as one of the main characters.

On this day, Sue was in her caravan going over her lines when there was a knock on her door telling her she was required on stage. Sue gathered her papers and walked to where the scene was being shot and waited on the outer parameter. The final actors were in position, including Rick Rodrigus, when an electrician moved a large flood light to put more light on centre stage. The actors were in position when suddenly the light tilted forward, breaking its two front legs as it entered free fall and came down on top of the main actor Rick Rodrigus, hitting him on the head and pinning him down as it lay on top of him. Everyone ran to assist to get the flood light off Rick, who was noticeably bleeding from his crushed head.

It took four men to lift the light off him. The director ran up to where he lay and turned him on his back to see if he was still alive. He wasn't breathing. He yelled out, 'Call an ambulance' and one assistant yells back, 'We have already done that. They should be here within five minutes.'

The ambulance arrived, and the paramedics grabbed their bag and ran to where the injured actor lay. They checked for a pulse. None could be felt. They declared him to be deceased and immediately called the police, who arrived shortly afterwards. The police noted what had happened and declared this was now a crime scene and no one was allowed on site until they had concluded their investigations, which should take a few weeks to complete.

The Director asked everyone to assemble away from the scene. He advised them that the police would not allow utilisation of the centre stage and because of that; it was necessary to stop filming for a month. A substitute would also need to be found to replace the principal actor, and all those scenes where Rick appeared would have to be filmed again. Everyone would have to go back home. They would be contacted when it was safe to come back on site.

The police asked questions about Rick Rodregus, and they were advised that he was not the most liked person on the set. Although he had a high opinion of himself, others did not share the same sentiment and provided unfavourable character references to the police. He was always getting into trouble or accusing everyone else of things they knew nothing about. He was disliked, and many thought he got what he deserved.

The police started to think this might have been an intentional act and not just an accident and probed further.

They found out that Rodregus owed money to a few people and had lost heavily in a card game. He also was reputed to have got one of the American Mafia's daughters pregnant and refused to marry her. The police continued their investigation.

Sue wondered what she was going to do for a month. She coincidentally received an email from the Monastery, asking for her help as they had been raided a few times and the army had left. Food that was for the children was taken, leaving the Monastery with very little provisions. Sue thought about it and decided to go and see for herself as to what the situation was.

She packed a bag. Booked her flight and before she knew it, was standing at the front door of the Monastery, greeting everyone.

She was taken to her room and allowed to unpack. At the airport, she hired a utility and packed it with as much food as she could. While she was unpacking her things, the nuns took the provisions from the utility into the kitchen and started preparing the meal for the children. Once cooked, all pitched in to feed the children who had not had a decent meal for days. The rest of the provisions were stored away in a basement storage area to ensure that if raided again, no one would find the supplies.

Sue was busy for a few days doing what Sister Mary used to do, taking care of those who attended the Monastery for ailments, injuries and food. She also gave directions to the nuns, making sure they attended to what was required to keep the Monastery opened. She wondered what would happen when she left, as no one seemed to have management skills to run the place.

Sue phoned her manager and found out that the police believed the light that fell on Rodregus killing him was no accident. The police were not allowing anyone on site for a further month. Sue ordered more supplies, which were air freighted in and again secured in the basement. All were paid for by the donations she arranged a year ago.

Sue again made friends with Timothy and Sarah and looked after them as a mother would look after her children. When it came time to leave, she knew it would be upsetting for all. She always had Timothy with her and washed and cared for Sarah, taking her outdoors into the sun so she could see how the other children played. She would always remember Rodney, but all indications were he was in a happy home and it would not be right to find out where he was or see him.

CHAPTER 9

Sue had been at the Monastery for about two weeks when one of the tribes raided it. They came into the Monastery looking for items to steal and went to the kitchen for food. The leader, named Arman Aarash from the Uzbek Tribe. They searched everywhere but could find nothing to steal that was of value. These men would kill anyone who got in their way by hitting them with the butt of their rifle or would just shoot the person dead. Life was of little value to them other than theirs.

Arman had everyone brought into the church and declared he wanted to know where they stored their provisions, as his men were hungry.

Sue told him all that they had was in the kitchen, and that was for the children. He didn't like Sue standing up to him and slapped her in the face with his opened hand, causing her to reel back and fall to the floor.

Arman was a tall man well built, around twenty-eight years of age. He came from the northern region and was educated by monks in a nearby church. His father was the head of the region and was renowned for his aggressiveness.

As there was nothing of value, he decided to take the wooden cross that stood at the front of the church. He made a movement towards the cross to see if there was going to be any objection to him stealing it, as it looked worthless. However, if someone objected then, that showed it was worth something.

Arman moved up to the cross and threw off the red cloth, which straddled both arms. At that time, the donkey came in and stood near the cross with his head down, ready to either make a charge at the tribesmen or kick him with his hoofs.

Arman stretched out his arms left and right to pick up the cross and pull it out from where it was anchored. As he did this, he was immediately held by the cross and screamed in agony. The donkey reared up and hit Arman in the back of his head with his hoof. Arman, while holding onto the cross, shook violently for about a minute and could not pull himself free from the cross. The donkey reared up again and was ready to deliver another blow when he stopped and waited as if someone was telling him not to attach Arman. Arman shook while screaming out and then fell to the floor beneath the cross, unconscious.

The nuns ran up to him while he laid on the floor and noticed his hands were burnt and bleeding. His face was radiant, but his arms were red as if scorched by fire.

His men picked Arman up off the floor and carried him to a pew at the front of the church and laid him down.

Sue ran up to him, thinking to herself, 'Well, you got what was coming to you, you bastard.' She looked at his hands, which were bleeding as if someone had pierced them with a sharp object. Both arms were bleeding, and blood was seeping from a hole in his left and right boot. She went to the office and brought back a medical kit and bandaged his wounds as best she could to ensure they did not become infected.

While Arman laid on the pew, his lieutenant grabbed the donkey and said, 'We can sell this animal and get some money for it. We will take it with us.' With that, he grabbed the donkey's main and yelled out to his men to bring a rope so he could put a noose around its neck.

While gripping the donkey, it suddenly turned and kicked the lieutenant with great force, sending him flying and landing several pews away. The Nuns and Sue ran up to him, but he was not breathing. More tribesmen ran into the church with guns and knives drawn. They ran up to their lieutenant and could see that he was dead. Two tribesmen looked at the donkey and moved towards him to throw a rope around his neck. The donkey reared up and hit the closest tribesmen in the forehead, sending him falling to the floor. The tribesman attempted to move past the donkey, but it kicked him in the face, and he fell backward. As he came down, the donkey gave him another kick to his legs, connecting both, causing the bones to shatter, crippling the tribesman. The donkey came up to where the tribesman laid and with one all almighty force landed both feet on the chest and head of the Tribesman killing him.

The donkey moved back to just being in front of the cross, making sure no one else made a move to remove it from the church.

Sue couldn't believe what she had seen. A donkey protecting a wooden cross. Why? What powers did the cross have and where did the donkey fit in?

By this time, Arman regained consciousness and tried to sit up. The nuns ran up to where he laid and assisted him to get up and stand. As he got up, he noticed his lieutenant straddled between two pews. He looked around and saw the cross and donkey. His men were planning to capture the donkey, but he commanded them not to and to leave the church immediately to prevent any theft from the Monastery. He went to where his lieutenant's body was and called his men to come and take it away. Then he sat down in a pew, trying to make sense of what had happened.

Sue walked up to him and offered him some water, which he took and drank. Sue says, 'What happened to you when you tried to take the cross?'

Arman said, 'The cross spoke to me. A voice said, I am the living resurrected God, Jesus Christ. The cross is the original cross on which I was crucified some three thousand years ago. All the pain and agony that was inflicted on me prior to being crucified and nailed to the cross you have felt through the cross. You have not felt the agony of all of man's sins which I bore on the cross. You shall be my minister at the Monastery and protect those who seek shelter there. I will protect you, but you will not live without pain.'

Arman said, ' I was crucified with Christ. I felt the whipping by the Roman soldiers and the pain as they nailed Jesus to the cross. This is why I shook as I could not bear the pain and suffering which was inflicted on Him. Towards the end, I was instructed on the interpretation of the bible and on church history and procedural matters.

Jesus has told me to become the head minister at the Monastery because the previous ministers were killed by tribesmen who attacked the place.

It seems there is going to be a lot of fighting around here, and Jesus has decided someone from the tribes would be best suited to ensure everyone stays alive. My men are to protect the Monastery and the children. You, I understand, will remain in charge of the orphanage and take over from Sister Mary.

Sue said, 'No, I am a film star, an actor and have a contract to fulfill. I make movies. I am not a social worker. Besides, I do not believe in God, so sorry I am leaving as soon as I know they are ready to resume making the film that I am currently working on. Where does the donkey fit into this? He attacked and killed your lieutenant. '

Arman said, 'My lieutenant was a very vicious man and has killed many in fights. He never worried about taking a life and now his life has been taken from him. The donkey was from the line selected by Jesus when he rode into Jerusalem on Palm Sunday. It has been the sole keeper of the cross and has taken it from place to place over the years. His predecessor was at the crucifixion and carried the dismantled cross from place to place under the direction and protection of Jesus. It is said that the cross has healing powers.'

Sue says, 'So if I took Sarah and placed her at the base of the cross, she would be healed. Is that what you are saying?'

Arman said, 'Who is Sarah? The cross will heal anyone who has faith in Jesus Christ.'

Sue looked at Arman and walked out of the church.

CHAPTER 10

Sue sat at her desk and was staring at an email from her manager. He advised her that the movie she was working on has decided not to resume and intends to seek a new lead man at the end of the year. They will contact her in a year's time to reschedule her availability once they have sourced a new lead actor. In the meantime, the movie in Portugal wants to shoot in a few weeks' time so she can make her way there and recommence her acting career. Sue wondered what Arman had said to her and that she would again have to leave Timothy and Sarah, who seemed to rely on her, especially Sarah.

She sat back in her chair and knew she had to make her mind up as to what she was going to do. It would not be right for her to just drift in and out of the children's lives. A decision had to be made, she either dropped them or took care of them, which of course requires money. She had no commitments before and was free to do anything she pleased or go anywhere. After thinking about it, Sue decided to go to Portugal and do her film and see what life brought her after that.

She went downstairs and into the church and waited for Armen to finish his discussion with a parishioner. As soon as he finished, she went up to him and advised him she would fly off to Portugal the next day to start a new movie. He was surprised as to her decision and said that to her. Sue then went to the kitchen and advised the sisters of her plans to fly to Portugal. They too were surprised as they thought she was happy about what she was doing and achieving for the community.

Sue then went to the orphanage and told Timothy and Sarah she would be leaving. They both burst into tears and were very upset for the rest of the day, especially Sarah, as she relied on Sue for all her needs. Timothy was at least mobile.

After sitting with the kids for an hour, Sue went to the kitchen to assist in the meal preparation for the evening. There were several sisters there, already attending to pealing vegetables while others were stirring pots that were on the stove.

The meal was cooked within an hour and placed on plates to feed the children. Sue went to help those children like Sarah who could not feed themselves.

Sarah didn't want Sue to feed her and refused to take any food she offered her. Another Sister had to help feed her, as Sarah was very upset to see Sue leave. Sue helped feed the other children and kept an eye on Sarah, who would not look at Sue. Once all the children were fed, the sisters attended to washing and drying the dishes and putting them away.

After finishing everything, the sisters sat down to eat and mainly talked about Sue leaving for Portugal. They were worried about managing without her because she handled most of the administrative work and decided what was to happen and when.

After a lot of discussion, Armen wished her all the best and got up and walked out, leaving the sisters to discuss things between themselves. He had a mass to handle that evening and went straight to church to prepare. One of his tribesmen advised him that a band of renegades were in the area and could try to gain entry to the Monastery. He placed his men at the outer perimeter to ensure any renegades would be spotted before trouble came their way. He then went to attend to the mass.

Halfway through the mass, Arman's men were attacked, and heavy gunfire was exchanged. Arman finished the mass quickly to ensure everyone could get home before the fighting erupted into a full-scale attack.

He then went to the front parameter and joined his men in repelling the attack. As he moved to a better position, one rebel spotted him and threw a grenade in his way, which exploded in front of him, knocking him out. They had to leave him as the rest of the men were under heavy gunfire and we're outnumbered. The fighting continued well into the night until most of the rebels were killed. The wounded rebels and those who surrendered were locked up in a disused jail near the monastery.

As soon as the fighting stopped, Sue went to see what had happened. She was concerned that Arman was injured and looked for him. Eventually, she located him amongst some dead bodies, barely breathing and with a wound seeping blood from his head. She immediately ordered some men to carry him to his room and went with them to attend to his injury. His head wound was sown to stop the bleeding, and Sue cleaned the rest of him as best she could. He really needed a bath, but she was not Florence Nightingale, so she would leave this for him to attend to once he regained consciousness.

The tribesman attended to the burial of the dead. Those men captured were released and allowed to return to their region on the understanding that they would be shot if they returned.

Things got back to normal. Arman regained consciousness after a day but was very weak and could not stand on his feet.

The Sisters attended to the daily masses, and Sue was waiting for Arman to get his strength back so she could make her way to Portugal and start her new film and continue with her career. She tried to see Timothy and Sarah, but Sarah just laid there, not looking at Sue. Timothy would run off and leave her alone. She got the message quickly that the children wanted nothing to do with her, as they felt she was going to abandon them. They thought they could trust her, but it turned out they couldn't as she would not look after them but cared only about her film career. They considered they were a novelty to her.

Arman was weak for about a week. He would try to get up but could not maintain his balance. Every time he got up, he just about fell. He got the idea quickly that he should stay in bed until his head wound got better. After a week, he could move around if he didn't overdo it. Eventually, he got back on his feet and could resume his normal duties.

CHAPTER 11

The hospital took shape, with all the buildings being fabricated and the fit-out well advanced. All the tradesmen completed their work and had returned to the States. The electronics were being connected and soon the facilities would undergo a test before being signed off as completed.

Sue decided to make her move to Portugal and advised the sisters of her plans. All were disappointed to see her go, but understood she wanted to resume her career as a film star.

She advised Arman of her plans, who was disappointed to see her go as she was managing the Monastery while he was injured. He had hoped she would continue allowing him to go to other regions preaching the word without worrying about the day-to-day issues of the Monastery.

Sue followed her normal daily routine. The hospital had been completed and was currently being audited to ensure it was fit for its purpose. It would soon take in patients. There were two doctors on hand and four nurses who were also trained to do minor surgery and attend to midwifery duties.

The marines were still on hand to ensure no one tried to raid the facilities. They were also backed up by helicopters, who could be called upon for support. Arman's men were also on hand to assist where needed.

A man arrived at the monastery in a truck one evening, requesting aid for his wounded men who had been attacked by tribesmen. The soldiers assisted them in taking the injured to the hospital. Once there, the so-called injured men pulled guns on the soldiers and ordered them to lay down their weapons. They then bound and gagged the soldiers and moved quickly and quietly to where the orphanage was located. The man held the sisters at gun point advising them they would shoot them and the children if they screamed for help. They ordered the sisters to take the children out of the orphanage and to wait outside of the monastery.

The Sisters obeyed the orders as they feared the men would shoot the children. Sue was standing outside the monastery when the sisters appeared with approximately thirty children. She asked what was happening just when one man grabbed her and pushed her in line. She screamed out, but the man hit her with the butt of his rifle, making her fall to the ground. He grabbed her by the throat, lifting her up. At that time, four trucks arrived, and the children, nuns and Sue were loaded into them, and they drove off.

It took some time before the soldiers were set free and raised the alarm of the kidnapping. Arman was advised, and he scrambled to his feet, still very groggy and unable to stand upright without leaning on things. He ordered his men to follow the trucks so as not to be seen and to report their location as soon as they knew where the children and nuns were being held.

After a couple of hours, they reported back that the men were from a northern tribe who intended to hold the children for ransom. That afternoon they appeared on television, declaring they would release their hostages upon payment of ten million dollars. It was not sure who was to pay the ransom as the region was managed by the tribes. As time went on, it became apparent that they viewed the Monastery as belonging to America, and they expected the American government to pay the ransom.

The American government declared it did not negotiate with extortionists and refused to pay the ransom. Behind the scenes, the Americans were planning on sending in a tactical team of Seals to free the hostages. A meeting was arranged with the Americans and Arman to establish a plan as to how best to achieve freeing the hostages.

CHAPTER 12

The children and nuns huddled together, fearing the worst. The tribesmen didn't seem to be educated men, just your basic scumbag tribesman, yet they were smart enough to pull this abduction off and to ask for ten million dollars. Sue thought about it and wanted to know who was behind the plan. She waited and after a couple of hours, a man appeared who seemed to be an American. She recognised him as a senator from one of the States in America.

The head of the tribe sat with the American Senator and Sue could see them arguing. The Senator wanted the tribesmen to kill hostages to show their seriousness and to pressure the Americans to decide quickly.

They agreed the Americans would be given twenty-four hours to decide and thereafter, two children would be executed each day until the ransom was paid. This was conveyed to the Americans who refused to pay the ransom. Everyone settled down for a long day. The children were fed with the little rations that were given to them and put to bed as soon as night came.

The next morning, the sisters made breakfast, but the children didn't eat it because the food wasn't edible. Most went hungry rather than to eat what was given to them.

A few hours afterwards, two tribesmen appeared and went through the children held captive. They selected two children who were to be executed that day. The execution would appear on YouTube to show the Americans that they were not kidding when they said they would kill two children a day until the ransom was paid.

Sue stood near the children as the tribesmen made their selection. One was a physically disabled girl who had surgery back in the States and who was gaining strength in her legs and would have been able to stop using her supports within a few months. The other child was Sarah, who could not move.

As soon as they selected Sarah, Sue let out with a scream yelling, 'Not Sarah. No, no.' She burst into tears as the men grabbed the first child and tried to take Sarah. Sue pushed them off Sarah just as one of them hit her in the face with the butt of his rifle, causing her to fall to the floor. They grabbed Sarah and lifted her off the bed just when Sue got to her feet.

Sue grabbed the gun from the tribesmen's belt and, without thinking, aimed the gun at the tribesmen and pulled the trigger. The bullet hit him in the head, and he dropped Sarah on the bed just as he fell to the floor. Blood was pouring out of his head. The other tribesman saw what had happened. He dropped the child he had in his arms and tried to reach for his gun. Sue expected this and shot him in the chest with a second shot to the head. Sue was tort as to how to use a gun in one of her films and this was second nature to her. The killing of someone was only temporary, as the victim in the movies always got up, whereas here they would not. She hoped they wouldn't.

Sue went up to the second tribesmen and took his gun and ammunition. She handed this to a sister to hold while she reloaded her own gun. Another sister moved forward and took the gun and said she knew how to use a gun as she had been brought up on a farm.

Both Sue and the sister went out of the room they were being held in to see what was happening. They could see the execution was to be televised as cameras were set up and that a meeting was taking place between the American Senator and the tribesman. It seems the Senator wanted them to get on with killing the children while the tribesmen did not want to carry out the killing. The tribesmen finally agreed to cut the throats of the children. The Senator was getting anxious and directed some men to see what was holding up the other two who were sent to get the two children.

Sue and the other sister brought the bodies into the room and hid them under the beds just before the tribesmen entered. The tribesmen looked around but could not see the first two men and assumed they went behind the building. So, they went there but could not find them. After about fifteen minutes, they came back in and selected two children for execution, one of which was Sarah. They tried to pick up the children and Sue grabbed her gun and fired at the tribesmen. He dropped Sarah and he fell to the floor. She then shot the second tribesmen as he was reaching for his rifle. As he leaned over trying to get his rifle, Sue shot him again, this time in the head, causing him to fall face down on the floor.

It was common to hear gunshots in the village, so no one was worried about the noise.

The head of the tribe became agitated, waiting for the children to be brought out, so he went to see for himself what was the holdup. He went to the room and opened the door and looked in but couldn't see any of his men, so he went outside behind the building but could not see where they were.

He came back in with another tribesman and ordered him to take a child, which he pointed out. At that time, he moved to take Sarah when Sue drew her gun and fired at him, hitting him in the heart, causing him to first lean over Sarah and then fall to the floor. The other sister drew her gun and shot the tribesman, who was going to pick up the second child. He fell immediately to the floor. The Sister quickly moved to where he fell, took his gun, rifle, and ammunition from him, and placed it at the foot of the bed where one child lay. She covered it up with a pillow so no one would see they had the weapons.

One tribesman, a second lieutenant, decided to see why his leader had not come out of the room where the children were being held in. He went to the door and opened it and could see his leader lying face down on the floor. Sue raised her gun and shot him in the chest as he tried to turn and run away. He fell to his knees, reaching for his rifle, and pointed it at Sue. She shot him a second time, but this time through the head, causing him to fall face down. They dragged him into the room and closed the door, hoping no one else would come.

The Senator became anxious as to why two children had not been brought out, so he got up and walked to the room where the children were being kept in. As he opened the door and looked in, he could see the dead bodies lying on the floor. He yelled out to the men for help, but as he tried to turn to run and get help, he was struck in the head by Arman and fell to the ground.

Other tribesmen sitting outside the headquarters upon hearing him scream got to their feet and moved to where the scream came from. As they turned, they were fired upon by the soldiers that came with Arman. They were killed while others raised their hands upon seeing that they were outnumbered and were surrounded.

Arman strapped the Senator's hands behind his back and went into the room. Sue immediately ran up to him, hugging him. She wouldn't let go until he said, 'Sue, enough. We have to hurry and load the children up onto the trucks before reinforcements come.'

Sue let go of Arman just when men came in to carry the children to the trucks. Arman's men and the marines stayed on guard outside to ensure that the rest of the tribe didn't start another shootout, which they would if they knew their leader was dead.

The children were loaded into the trucks and the others got into whatever vehicle they could find for the journey back to the Monastery.

Sue found herself sitting with Arman in the truck. She still had her rifle and two guns with her, which she intended to keep just in case there was another attempt by the warlords in the area.

Sue and Armen began talking, with Sue telling Arman what had happened when they were kidnapped and how they were brutely handled and that she was forced to shoot the tribesmen to stop them from taking Sarah and killing her.

Arman pointed out to Sue that it was a sin to kill, and she should seek God's forgiveness for what she believed was necessary.

Sue said, 'You must be joking. I don't believe in God as he never supports his believers.'

Arman said, 'Why do you say that? Something must have happened in your life that has caused you to think that way or to have turned from God.'

Sue says, 'Yes, it did. When I was eight, both parents died because of a road accident, and I was forced into foster care. When I finished school, I took up a job as a retail assistant and was spotted by a producer who gave me a chance to develop a career in films. I prayed to God to save my parents as I relied on them for everything, but he did nothing to help. My mother died in extreme pain. God did nothing but showed he was a fence sitter not willing to help.'

Arman said, 'I don't think so. It seemed you idolised your parents and did not believe in God. God removed the idols from your life and showed you how little you believed in Him. We must all die, and your parents died when their time had come. How did you become a film star?'

Sue says, 'I guess I was lucky. I couldn't afford to go to university when I finished school, so I was able to get a retail position at Walmart. One day, I was serving in the lady's garment section when a producer came up to me to buy a dress for her daughter. I never came across a female producer before and asked questions and got to know her as time went on. A month later, she came to the store to see me and said she had a minor part in a film if I was interested. I jumped at the opportunity. She put me through an eight-week course in drama school and then on the set she advised what she wanted from me. I did well in the part, and she used me in other movies until I learnt how to act. Many other actors would pass on tips which I took on board and over the years my minor parts became major parts, and I now have become recognised in many countries.'

Arman said, 'Don't you think that was part of God's plan for you?'

Sue says, 'I don't think so. He wouldn't care what happened to me.'

Arman said, 'I wouldn't be too sure about that. You will have to find your way back to God. You know that the cross that transformed my life can help Sarah.

Sue says, 'I know what it did to you because I was there and saw it. But I don't think God is interested in me. Anyhow, I must finish a film in Italy as soon as we get back.'

Arman said, 'So you intend to leave Sarah again? You know she thinks you as her mother?'

Sue said, 'Yes, I know, but I have a contract that I must fill, otherwise they will take legal action against me.'

Arman said, 'Then what are you going to do.?

Sue said, 'I will check with the producer to see when they need me and make plans from there. You will look after Sarah for me while I am away, won't you?'

Arman said, 'I will do my best, but if we come under a further attack, I am required to defend the Monastery and not just one child.'

Sue said, 'What would happen to Sarah if I placed her under the cross? Would God heal her?'

Arman said, 'You see, you say you do not believe in Christ, yet you want Him to perform a miracle for you as if he is obligated to do. Just to satisfy you. You know at the Cross they kept yelling out show us a sign and we will believe in you. He raised a man from the dead, Lazarus, yet they still did not believe in him. He made the blind see yet again they did not want to believe in Him.

It is doubtful that you will believe in Him as your heart has turned against Christ. Sarah will never get better because of your nonbelief. You see, a nonbeliever cannot find favouritism with Christ on the basis you do this for me, and I will believe.

Faith is not battering. So, when the matter is done, you stop believing? No, belief in Christ is more than a stop and start situation or bargaining. What you should have said in pray when your parents died is, Lord, I don't understand why you have allowed both my parents to be taken from me, but I believe in you and rest my life in your hands. I am sure over time you will show me why I had to go through this hardship and trauma.'

Sue says, 'Well, I didn't and cannot find the feelings to do that. I guess I will have to see if I can fix Sarah medically.'

Arman said, 'You tried that, and everyone has told you it cannot be done as her central nervous system has been damaged during the operation, forcing her to be paralysed for life from the neck down.'

Sue says, 'Yes, I agree, but I will still look to see if any modern invention can help Sarah. I cannot find God in my heart and still believe he will not help me. Yes, I believe what you have said as I have seen what has happened to you and other children placed at the foot of the Cross, but while I believe there is a God, I don't think he cares about me.'

The trip took a long time, and everyone was happy to be home once they pulled up outside the Monastery. The children were let out of the trucks to play, while the soldiers stood guard at the Monastery's perimeter to prevent any attacks. In the evening, the children were bathed and fed and put to bed.

The Senator was arrested and placed in a jail for return flight to the States to face a trial of kidnapping with intent to murder.

Sue drew closer to Sarah after the ordeal and Sarah understood Sue had saved her life.

Sue contacted her agent, who was very anxious to hear from her. He made arrangements for her to fly to Italy so she could attend to her obligation as the lead role in the film.

A tearful Sue said goodbye to Sarah and Timothy and assured them she would be back as soon as she had finished the film. It was unspecified how long she would be gone, which could range from four to six months, depending on the weather and the availability of actors with roles in the film.

Sue said goodbye to the sisters she had gotten to know and gave them her contact details in case they needed to talk to her. Each one of them received a kiss and a hug from her, which seemed to last forever.

Sue said her goodbyes to Arman and gave him a big hug before she got into the car that was going to drive her to the airport.

CHAPTER 13

Sue sat back in her seat, wondering what was being said about her back at the Monastery. Despite having no real claim on them, she continued to think about Sarah and Timothy as if they were her own children, knowing that anyone with a home and a desire for a family could adopt them.

While falling asleep, her mind wandered to the conversation she had with Arman and his thoughts on faith and belief. She knew she was falling in love with Arman, even though she tried to get him out of her mind. She was startled by a flight attendant tapping her on the shoulder, telling her to belt up and put her seat in an upright position, as they were going to land soon.

The plan landed without incidence and a car was waiting at the airport to take her to the studio. One hour later, she was on the set viewing some actors going through their lines. The director yells out, 'Ready this is a live shot! Quite please. Action.' The actors performed their parts and fifteen minutes later, the director yells out, 'Cut. Perfect. We will go with this shot.'

The production had worked around Sue while she was held captive by the tribesmen, which meant they were not behind in their schedule.

Sue went to her caravan and saw her costume was on her bed. She also noted her suitcase was on the table and there were a few unexpected items there, such as a bunch of flowers in a vase on a shelf which enlightened the room. While Sue was admiring the flowers, there came a knock at the door and a voice yelled out, 'Are you decent?' Sue opened the door, and her assistant stood there with a big smile on her face. She says to Sue, 'Good to see you back in one piece. I am here to help you dress as they want you on the set within an hour. Make-up is waiting for you, so we must hurry. I will put your things away while you're filming.'

Sue let her assistant in, and both went to the back of the caravan. She took her clothes off and her assistant helped her get dressed. Ten minutes later they were heading to makeup. Sue was shown a chair where they wanted her to sit, and a group of people worked on her. First, they put her makeup on and then attended to her hair and arms to ensure she looked the part in the film. Once everyone was happy with her appearance, she was escorted to the stage to wait her turn.

Sue went through her lines and the director advised what he was looking for. A further rehearsal was done, and the director showed he was happy with what he saw. They again went on stage, but this time the acting would be filmed and the take the final one.

Director yells out, 'Action.'

Each of the actors went through their lines until the director yelled out "Cut'. They then moved off the set to enable the next scene to be moved in and the old scenery moved out.

This went on for the rest of the day until the last scene was shot for the day. Everyone could then go to the canteen and have dinner or go out and bring something back to be eaten later.

CHAPTER 14

Arman started the day with mass but knew something was not right. There were more people than usual, and the congregation consisted predominately of men, and most with beards indicating a tribal upbringing. Arman did not let on that he was concerned, but halfway through the mass, he acted as if he was out of incense and had to get more. He went to where the army lieutenant was stationed and advised him of the possibility of a skirmish in the church. Troops were secretly positioned outside the church and some in plain clothes were stationed inside. As predicted, soon after Arman returned, some men drew their weapons and started shooting at those present in the church.

Arman fell to the floor and drew his pistol and returned fire, killing two of the tribesmen. The other men brought in also immediately drew their weapons and shot as many tribesmen as they could. The troops outside stormed in and the remaining tribesmen quickly surrendered when they saw they were outnumbered.

Once the skirmish was over, the lieutenant went to where Arman fell and turned him over. He had been shot, and it appeared the bullet was close to if not in the heart. He ordered his men to take Armen to the operating theatre, and a surgeon was informed of what had happened.

Armen was sedated and immediately operated on. The bullet had lodged a quarter of an inch away from the heart in a muscle near the heart. The surgeons removed the bullet and gave Arman a blood transfusion, as he had lost a lot of blood. After the operation, Arman was placed in the ward and was placed under observation around the clock. He was sedated for twenty-four hours and then allowed to regain consciousness.

With Arman out of action, there was no one in charge and therefore a lot of the security was left unattended to. This would mean that the Monastery was vulnerable if a further attack happened.

Nicholas and the nuns would take it in turn to do mass, but Sunday normal sermons were handled by Nicholas until Arman could get back on his feet.

The nuns emailed Sue to advise her of the raid and that Arman was shot and hospitalised after he underwent an operation to remove a bullet close to his heart.

Arman did not get better and, in fact, got worst after his operation, which mystified the doctors as they thought all went well when they operated on him. His temperature spiked to a dangerous level, prompting the doctors to arrange for an exploratory operation to see what had gone wrong.

Sue was informed of Arman's declining condition and of the need to operate again to see what was causing the high temperature and preventing Arman from getting better.

The doctors placed Arman on a course of antibiotics, which were administered intravenously, to reduce his temperature. They thought his wound got infected, which caused his high temperature and increased his blood pressure, putting him at risk of a heart attack or stroke.

CHAPTER 15

Sue read her emails, which made her quite concern as to what was happening at the Monastery. She was alarmed to read that Arman was not getting better but worst after his operation to remove the bullet from near his heart. She was also concerned about Sarah as to who was looking after her to ensure she didn't give up hope of getting better one day.

Sue asked the producer for a week off to help the Monastery, but the producer said no because they needed her to finish filming, which would take a few more weeks.

Over time, Sue received more emails about Arman's condition getting worse. Doctors planned a further operation to find the source of the infection.

Sue again tried to convince herself that it had nothing to do with her and that she was a film star doing a movie, not an administrator of the Monastery. Since she didn't adopt Sarah and Tim, they weren't her problem. She should forget about them and concentrate on the film she was acting in.

Sue was in her caravan, practicing her lines for tomorrow, when she heard that an actor she knew had been criticised for bad acting in a movie. This criticism made it difficult for him to find more work and make a living. She reflected on this and knew of other actors who had the same experience in not getting the ratings and therefore were overlooked for future roles.

She debated whether it was better to fake belief in a God she didn't believe in or face challenges as an actor with bad reviews and limited job opportunities. Sue, of course, didn't think that God controlled everything and could ensure she made the right decision. This, of course, never entered her mind.

Sue decided to take the risk and not go back to the Monastery, but to concentrate on her film career. She was abruptly brought out of her thinking by a knock at the door of her caravan and got up and opened the door to see who was there. As she opened the door, she could see the producer standing there and invited him in. As he came in, Sue noticed he was accompanied by another person who was hanging onto some medical equipment.

The producer advised that some actors had come down with Covid and had been hospitalised and that all the actors were to be tested. Initially by a RAT test and if it showed positive, a pathology lab test. She agreed to be tested and allowed the nurse to swob her nose and throat and then test her sample. She proved negative and was advised that they would film her scenes over the next two days, which would then allow her nine days off until she was next required. Sue agreed to the schedule and immediately advised the Monastery that she was allowed a few days off and could come there to assist them.

Over the next two days, Sue concentrated on acting her scenes. The actors with Covid were kept in isolation in the ICU at the local hospital and put on respirators. They said they would be out for a week, but it was uncertain how long it would take since Covid affected everyone differently.

Sue had already booked her flight and had her bags packed to ensure she did not waste any time once she had completed filming her scenes. She made sure that all her scenes were shot, which left only a few scenes that had to be filmed with one or two of the other actors.

Before she knew it, she was in the air on her way to the Monastery. After landing, she caught a taxi to the Monastery and arrived in the afternoon. All the sisters warmly welcomed her, but Sarah and Tim kept their distance because they thought she would only be here briefly and then leave again.

Sue went to the hospital to check on Arman's condition and could see he was not doing well. The doctors decided to operate on him again the next morning to see what was causing the infection. The antibiotics did not seem to help much, and he was administered morphine to ease his pain.

Sue sat near Arman and put her hand in his, hoping he would sense she was near. He gripped her hand, which showed he could still sense her presence. She sat there for about thirty minutes, holding his hand and talking to him. Her thoughts drifted, and she found herself saying things that she would never have said to Arman directly. He gripped her hand to show he agreed. She was not sure whether she proposed marriage or what but got up and leaned over and gave him a kiss on his forehead and left him.

Sue went back to the Monastery and straight to the office to check the records as to what was happening. Over the time she had been away, there were fifteen newly born babies left at the Monastery gates which the orphanage had to take in and try to find homes for. They had established a connection with some agencies in different countries who could find a home for the orphans. The procedure was to keep the babies for ninety days to give the mother time to come in and claim their babies, which happened in twenty-five percent of the time. The other babies were left in the orphanage as the parent could be a single mother and did not want the responsibility of looking after them or, as most was the case, they could not afford to feed another mouth.

Some mothers gave birth at the clinic and left the babies at the hospital for adoption again, not able to provide for their newborn. There were a few who had phycological issues and therefore could not keep the baby. Full term was preferred to aborting the baby as this was seen as killing. This way, some couple who could not have a baby managed to get one and start a family with one or two adoptions.

The township discovered the clinic could meet most of their medical needs, so more and more patients started coming for treatment. The number of beds in the ward filled up quickly, requiring the hospital to open their second ward one year before schedule.

Sue observed that the hospital's funding came from the interest and dividends earned on the initial donations invested with professional bodies in the US.

After spending some hours at the office, Sue went to the church and sat in one pew and said a pray for the speedy recovery of Arman. She sat there for about ten minutes looking at the cross and the number of people that stopped and prayed in front of it. Some would place their babies at the foot of the cross and prayed, while others would pray holding onto their babies.

As she sat there, the donkey came in, when no one was before the cross, and bowed before the cross and stood there for a minute and went. She was fascinated by the dedication by the donkey and thought that if the donkey believed in the cross and Jesus, then what is stopping her from believing?

Her life rarely required God as he had in her eyes proven incapable of helping those in need but instead made things somewhat worse. The poor did not get richer but were exploited by the rich who took advantage of them and robbed them of what little money they had. So, money and possessions must not count, otherwise the rich would get first preference before God, and they don't. So, what was it that made the difference? It must be the promise of internal life which is promised to those who believe in Jesus Christ.

Sue got up and went back to her desk to finish some of the administrative work that had not been attended to. She finished this in about an hour and then went to check on Sarah.

No one had taken her out of her bed nor gave her any attention. Sue picked her up and took her outside to allow her to see what it was like outside. Tim came by and gave Sarah a kiss, and she smiled. Sue noticed Sarah was not happy and would not sit up when placed in that position. She was worried and took her to the clinic to get her checked out.

After waiting half an hour, one doctor became free and was happy to check Sarah out. He had seen her before and from the outset also noted she was not responding to things that were said to her. After examining Sarah, the doctor believed she was becoming withdrawn because of her restriction and reliance on other people. He believed she would soon die from the condition if her mental state did not change. This alarmed Sue, who didn't know what to do. The doctors could only recommend antidepressants, but Sue would not agree to Sarah having to take them. She thanked the doctor and took Sarah back outside, where the other children were playing. One nun came out to check on the children and Sue asked her to keep an eye on Sarah, as she wanted to check on Arman.

She walked a couple of floors rather than use the elevator and went into Arman's room. He was still running a temperature, and Sue was concerned as to the cause. She sat there for about ten minutes when a bed was wheeled into his room and a couple of nurses came in to lift Arman onto the bed. Sue asked what was happening and was told that Arman was to be operated on in about an hour's time to see what was causing the high temperatures.

Arman was shifted onto the bed, and they wheeled him away. Sue stopped them and leaned over Arman and gave him a kiss on the forehead and squeezes his hand to let him know she was there.

They took Arman to the operating theatre, and after sedating him, began the operation. One hour later, the surgeon came out to the waiting room to speak to Sue. They had found that the bullet that they took out last time was not totally removed and fragments were left in his chest which caused the infection.

The doctor assured Sue that they had removed all the fragments this time, and that Arman would now make a speedy recovery. He was left in preop for another hour and after the anaesthetist was happy with his condition, was wheeled back to his room and transferred into his own bed and allowed to sleep off the anaesthetic. Sue went in after they transferred Arman into his own bed and sat there waiting for some movement to make sure he was coming out of the anaesthetic. As she sat there, she wondered how a triable leader became a servant of God, and through the cross gained the knowledge he did about the bible and what had happened to Jesus on the cross. He was now an apostle. At the time he tried to lift the cross up, he felt the full pain Jesus had felt on the cross and the knowledge of the Bible was passed onto him through Christ.

After about an hour, Arman woke up and opened his eyes, not sure he was seeing well as he saw Sue sitting there and thought it was a mirage. He put out his hand to touch her, to just confirm it was her. He slowly regained consciousness and asked Sue questions as to how long he had been in a coma as he remembered nothing except dreaming Sue was around him. He remembered her kisses and squeezing his hand, her saying a pray over him which he thought was unusual as she said she did not believe in God.

The monitor Arman was attached to showed he had a high blood pressure, a reduced oxygen level and an increasing temperature, which baffled the doctors. They took all the bullet fragments out from his chest and made sure that there was nothing remaining that could cause his temperature to rise to the level it had.

Sue sat with Arman for a further half an hour as he dosed off to sleep. She left him to attend to some of her duties at the orphanage as one mother of a newborn baby wanted to reclaim her baby, which was left at the front door of the church two days before. It wasn't difficult to locate her baby, as it was the only boy left at the front of the church. All the other babies were girls. In fact, most of the babies left were girls. It was rare a boy would be handed over to the orphanage.

Sue sat with the mother and advised her of the procedure they would have to follow before they can hand any baby over to her. First, she would have to do a DNA check, and the result compared to the hospital's records to ensure the correct baby was being handed over. Second, she would have to prove she had the means to take care of the baby and third, she had to undergo a medical examination to ensure she was in reasonable health. The women agreed to these conditions and a blood sample was taken from her to check on the match.

What transpired was her DNA matched a baby girl's DNA and not the boy they thought was hers. In discussing this with her, she advised her husband did not want a girl and would refuse to allow the girl to live. The women brought the girl to the orphanage knowing her husband would kill the baby girl. If she told him they had a boy, he would be pleased and allow the boy to live. This is why she was claiming the boy was hers.

Sue could not release the boy into her care and the mother refused to take her baby girl back, as she knew her husband would kill the baby. Sue refused to allow her to take any of the children and she left empty handed. The baby girl was adopted by a couple who could not have children and after two years, they adopted a baby boy into their family. The mother left the clinic without a child and was never seen of again.

Sue decided to check on Arman to see how he was getting on. She went to his room and noticed he had a high temperature and blood pressure. The doctors could not determine the cause of his high temperature, despite removing all the fragments in the previous operation. Arman received a blood transfusion with a matching blood type, which was checked regularly before being administered. The doctors were concerned that Arman would end up with a stroke if his temperature was not lowered. They decided to put him in an ice bath, which should stabilise his temperature. Everything was prepared and Arman was lowered into the bath and left there for an hour. His temperature was stabilised but at a high level. He could shower after an hour and was then returned to his room.

Sue came in just as they were putting Arman back into his bed. He was weak and needed help for any task that required exertion. She could see that things were not going right and that, if not fixed, would cause Arman's death. As she sat there looking at Arman, Sue decided to take Arman before the cross, as others have done in the past. Arman was not hooked up on any drip or monitors yet, so now would be the best time. She went down the hall and found a wheelchair and took it to Arman's room. Sue woke Arman up and got him into the wheelchair and threw a blanket over him and set off to the church, which was next to the hospital.

The church was empty, and no one was working inside. Sue maneuvered the wheelchair as close as she could and within reach of the cross. Arman, seeing what Sue was doing, looked at her as if to say, 'What are you thinking? You don't believe in God', but she was doing it for him as he believed. Arman stretched out his hands and as he touched the cross, could feel all the illness being drained from his body and his temperature going down. After a few minutes, he let go of the cross and sat back in his wheelchair and said a pray thanking the Lord for answering his prays. Sue, who was close by, could not believe what she had witnessed. She could see that Arman had been cured and while still weak, could sit in the wheelchair unaided.

Sue immediately put the blanket over Arman and took him back to his room. She helped him get out of the wheelchair and back into bed just as if nothing had happened. She took the wheelchair back to the place she found it and returned to Arman's room. Both looked at each other, not sure what to say. Eventually Arman spoke. He says, 'What are we going to tell the doctors?'

Sue says, 'Nothing. What is there to say that a miracle happened, and you have been cured?' Just as Sue spoke, a doctor came into Arman's room and wired him up to the monitors. As he was doing this, he noticed all the readings were normal and paged the senior medical officer, who arrived a few minutes later.

The medical officer was happy that all the monitors showed normal readings and could only attribute it to Arman's ice bath. Arman knew better, but Sue still had doubts, but neither let on as to what really happened. The doctors medically examined Arman and allowed him to resume his normal duties if he took things slowly.

After a day of resting, Arman resumed his duties, and Sue could again leave the Monastery to go back to Portugal to finish her film.

CHAPTER 16

Sue sat in her caravan waiting to be called up for her last scene. It was two months since she left the Monastery, and she was glad to have the move completed.

Her agent emailed her to notify her he had secured a part for her in another move, which would shoot in three months' time in Italy. The role would give her a chance to showcase her acting skills and potentially win an award. The cast included established actors, and the producer had a history of winning awards.

Her mind flashed back to the Monastery and the miracle she witnessed with Arman. None of the doctors could do what the cross did for Arman and his condition no doubt deteriorated to the extent that she could only turn to God for help, for there was no one else capable of curing Arman. But Sue still had doubts, even after witnessing his miraculous cure. She kept thinking 'Show me a sign.'

Sue didn't know what to do regarding the next movie. Despite Arman's assurance that he would look after Sarah, she still wondered what was happening with her. She felt that her soul was compelling her to go back to the Monastery, yet it was always hard to come away from there. She realised she was not the glamour girl she once was and that she would have to make up her mind what she wanted from life. A film career or a wife and or a mother to two adopted children. She had kept up to date with the children through Zoom with Arman's help. Sue spoke with Arman each day and the children, which they were glad to hear from her.

During the daily conversation with Arman, she put the idea to him to place Sarah at the foot of the cross and ask the Lord to cure her. No medical surgeon seemed to have the will to operate on her because of the proximity of the damage to the central nervous system. Arman was all for it, but question Sue's wavering belief in God.

Unless Sue believed in the Lord and had faith, nothing would come from the trial. Sue saw what the belief in the Lord can do, but still was hesitant. She could not see why the Lord took her parents away from her when she was still relatively young. As Sue was deep in thought, there was a knock at the door and a voice yelled out, 'You're wanted for the last shot'.

Sue was ready and walked to the stage where she was to perform her final act to finish the movie. The cast in the previous shot were still on hand as the Director was not happy with the way it turned out. He decided to shoot this scene again and wanted the cast to go through their motions again before the last filming. Sue stayed on to see what the problem was. The group assembled and acted their parts. The Director pulled them up on things he thought were not appropriate and made suggestions which would satisfy him. The cast assembled and went through their roles and finally the Director was happy and advised he would use this scene in the last cut.

Sue was next on stage and each of the actors went through their routine until the Director was satisfied with what they were going to present as a last cut. The cameras were rolling and twenty minutes later the Director yells out 'Cut' and everything was concluded. Everyone could wait around for another month to see if they were required to repeat a scene or could go off home and come back if required.

Sue decided to go to the Monastery rather than hanging around and booked her flight for the next day.

She got up early the next day and made her way to the airport just to find out that her flight had been cancelled owing to the bad weather on route. She rebooked on the next available flight and went back to her unit, hoping she could fly out tomorrow.

Sue had an early night, hoping to get an early flight the next day.

The next morning, Sue called to check if her flight was on time. She was informed that heavy rain in the area meant it was unlikely she could leave until two days later. She phoned Arman and set up a Zoom session to have a face-to-face meeting with him and the children. They were all happy to see each other but concerned as to when Sue could get to the Monastery.

The next day, things had improved to the degree that Sue's flight was rescheduled, and she could take off on time on the third day.

CHAPTER 17

Sue arrived at the Monastery and was greeted affectionally by all. Arman was very happy to see her and gave Sue a big hug and a kiss. Timothy came over and got a big kiss. Sarah was nowhere in sight, so Sue went to the orphanage and could see no one was looking after her. She took her outside and sat her up in a wheelchair so she could see all the other children playing and she was very happy to be out of the bed.

That evening, over dinner, Sue approached the possibility of placing Sarah under the cross with the view that the Lord would heal her.

Arman was not keen on it as he didn't think Sue had enough faith in God and, therefore, nothing would come of it. Sue's attitude was that we should try all things, and she thought that if both were present, Sarah would be healed. It was agreed that they should put Sarah under the cross the next day at about midday as there would be the least number of people praying in church and they did not want to create a movement which would build up anticipation amongst those present that God would automatically heal Sarah. If He didn't, then this could lead to those present to turn from God, as no doubt the thought would be that if there was a God, he would have cured Sarah.

They finished their meal and, after attending to the chores, all ended up going to bed early. The next morning, everyone was busy attending to their work commitments. Midday came quickly and before everyone knew it was time to assemble in church to see if God would cure Sarah.

Sue went to the orphanage and picked Sarah up and brought her into the church. To her surprise, the church was full of Nunns and churchgoers who had heard that a miracle was in the making. It seems that the Nuns sitting at the dinner table spread the word as to what was going to happen, and people came from everywhere to bear witness to the miracle. In fact, there was not enough room inside the church, so most had to wait outside and could not see what was happening.

Sue moved to where Arman was sitting. She was worried that so many people came but could not refuse to allow them entry into the church. It was unfortunate that most were not believers and thought that if Sarah was cured, I might believe in God. Otherwise, nothing lost except a few hours, and I will carry on with my life the way I have in the past, knowing there is no God.

Sue gave Sarah to Arman, who took her and said a pray over Sarah. He then laid her at the foot of the cross and with Sue kneeled before the cross. Arman said a pray while Sue looked on. They then left Sarah and went back to their pew and waited.

The donkey came in and seeing Sarah at the foot of the cross, moved closer to her. He could see she could not move and stood there for about two minutes. He then kneeled before the cross and walked out.

Arman went to where Sarah laid and picked her up. He carried her to where Sue was sitting and handed Sarah to Sue. Sue could see that nothing had been done to cure Sarah and was very disappointed. She sat there for five minutes and took Sarah back to the orphanage and put her back in her bed and walked out to her office.

All in the church started to talk amongst themselves, saying, 'There is no God. God would have cured the child. He would at least showed us a sign, but there was nothing proving he is a myth. Doesn't exist. Just a man-made fabrication.'

As Sue sat in her room thinking about what had happened, Arman walked in. She turned to him and said, 'Well, that was a waste of time, wasn't it? Most came to at least get a sign but got nothing but proof that this believe stuff is just a myth. Another way of getting the poor to contribute to a rich church.'

Arman replied, 'The problem is with you. You have seen the miracles God has done, but you still do not believe in Him. What you and the crowd are saying is if you God perform magic for us, we will consider whether we should believe in you, otherwise we will remain non-believers. Jesus does not care whether you believe in him. He is trying to save you from yourself. He wants you to know that he is the only way through which your sins will be forgiven. Unless he forgives your sins, you can never appear before God and therefore, will not have an internal life. You have to pray to Jesus asking Him to show you the way and to overcome your hesitancy in accepting Him.'

Sue looked at Arman and walked out of her office, knowing what Arman said was right, but still found it hard to believe in Jesus. She went to the orphanage and collected Sarah and took her into the playground and sat Sarah in a wheelchair so she could see the other children. After sitting there for about an hour, she took Sarah back to her bed as she had work to do and needed time to attend to some urgent matters. She noticed there was a note on her desk from Arman advising he was going to some villages to preach the gospel and would be away for about a month. Because of most of the villages were Moslems, she believed it wouldn't be a good idea as conflict would arise when Arman attempted to convert them. She headed to Arman's room to try to change his mind.

Arman was not in his room or in his office so Sue went to the church where he was talking to some parishioner about an abortion and was trying to convince the mother to have the baby and if after birth she could not look after the baby, the orphanage would take it and place the baby up for adoption. The mother seemed agreeable, but her hot-headed partner wanted her to have an abortion. You could see that the husband didn't care about the baby or the mother. All that counted was the opinion of his village and those in authority. He kept yelling, 'No, we have an abortion now. Not later. Now, while thumping his fist on the pew he was sitting in.

Arman made it clear the mother can give birth at the hospital so no one would know what had happened. But no matter what he said, the husband was against it. Finally, they could not come to terms with a plan that they all agreed to, so the two left the church with the matter unresolved.

Sue waited until the couple had left and then approached Arman about preaching the word to the surrounding villages. She argued with him, and he could see she would not let him go by himself. He advised that some men from his village will accompany him, and they will protect him. He was against her accompanying him, as he could get out of trouble by himself without worrying about her safety. Also, he did mention there may be a possibility she would need to go back to finish her movie if they needed to retake some scenes again. The argument went back and forth until Arman finally said, 'I will be under the protection of Jesus Christ.' That was a red rag to a bull. Sue said, 'Are you joking? He would even cure Sarah, let alone prevent you from being shot.'

Arman pointed out that, in normal circumstances, he could not do his work of spreading the word of Jesus Christ. While she was at the Monastery, he could focus on spreading the gospel, as she would take care of running the Monastery and looking after Sarah.

Sue still didn't like it, as she knew there would be a lot of danger involved but understood there was no way she could change his mind.

While Sue and Arman were arguing, Nicholas came in to advise them a pregnant woman was found alongside the road with a bullet in her chest. She was taken to the hospital where the surgeons were going to operate on her to see if they could save her life and the baby.

The operation went on for about two hours and the doctors declared she would live, and the baby had not been harmed. Both Arman and Sue went down to see her, but she was still very much under the anaesthetic and could not tell them as to what happened.

The next day, they tried to see her and were allowed entry by the head nurse. They asked a lot of questions and found out that her husband didn't intend for to have an abortion. He always had the idea of killing her rather than for her to have an abortion. He had shot her thinking he shot her through the heart, making her death a certainty.

Arman decided to pay the man a visit and took some of his men with him, just in case there was trouble. After travelling for two hours, they arrived at the village the man lived in. Despite asking for him, no one knew his whereabouts but was informed of his place of residence. They went to his house, but it was locked, and it seemed no one had been there for some time. They went to speak to his neighbours, who were unwilling to speak about him other than to say he was a very violent man who thought nothing of killing someone.

Armen went to the local hotel to see if he was there. He walked in with two of his men and sat down to see if they could spot him. After about ten minutes, a group of men walked in and one of them was the man they were looking for. They went up to the bar and ordered drinks and sat at a table near to where Arman was sitting. They were vociferous and did not care what other patrons thought of them.

Armen waited until the man they wanted went to the bathroom. He followed him in and confronted the man accusing him of shooting his pregnant wife and leaving her by the roadside. The man immediately withdrew a knife from his belt and tried to stab Arman with it, intending to kill him. Arman expected this and hit the man in the face, sending him to the floor. The tribal leader got up, still with the knife in his hand. He lunged at Arman, cutting him on the arm. Arman grabbed his hand that held the knife and turned it to point at the man's throat. The man resisted and during the struggle slipped on a wet spot on the bathroom floor with the knife penetrating his throat and severing an artery. Blood poured out onto the floor and as Arman let go of the man, he fell face down on the floor in his pool of blood.

Arman washed his hands and wrapped a hanky over his arm to stop it from bleeding. He walked out of the bathroom to his table and singled for his men to follow him out of the hotel, which they did. Outside, he advised them what had happened and to be prepared for a shootout with the tribesmen. They positioned themselves away from the hotel and waited. Sure enough, they came out looking for revenge and sighting them down the road ran towards the group they recognised were sitting at a table near them at the hotel a few moments ago.

As the tribesman ran towards Arman's men, they began shooting without first finding out who they were shooting at and whether they were the ones who killed their leader. They didn't care as long as someone paid for the killing.

The group being shot at raised their rifles and returned fire, killing all the confronting tribesman. In the town, no one cared about law and order, and most matters were handled by mob rule.

Arman ordered his men to load the dead men into their vehicle and take them to the undertaker for burial. Once they off loaded the bodies, they hosed their utility down and set off for home before more trouble followed them.

It was dark when Arman drove into the Monastery. He went to his room and had a shower, washing the blood off his arm. He knelt near his bed and prayed, asking for forgiveness for his sin of killing the tribesman at the hotel. As he prayed, he realised his selection as an apostle was because of his knowledge of the area, strength, and fighting capabilities. He finished dressing and went down to the kitchen to see if he could get something to eat. His men were already there, and a meal had been prepared for them. He sat down and had his dinner and was ready to get up when Sue walked in and asked how things went. He advised her that all the men were killed and would not trouble the Monastery or others anymore.

After the meal, Arman went to church to attend to late night mass and once completed, went to his room to rest. A few minutes passed when there was a knock at the door. He got up and opened it. Sue was there and asked whether she could come in? He let her in, and she sat in the chair while he sat at his desk. She wanted to know what had happened as she was going to the hospital to see how tribesman's wife was getting on and wanted to know what to say to her. Arman went with her so he could tell her what had happened to her husband.

They went to the ward the woman was in and approached her bed. She noticed them and immediately began talking to them. Arman and Sue greeted her and sat near her bed. Arman advised her that her husband was dead, and all his men were killed in a shootout. She was not surprised as her husband was always shooting or killing someone and she knew some day his turn would come. At least now he would not have another chance to kill her. She decided now that her husband was dead, to return to her village and have her baby and would take care of the baby herself and not give it up for adoption.

Sue and Arman left her and went back to Arman's office at the Monastery to discuss what was next. Arman advised Sue that he intended to go to some villages and preach the word of Christ, as did Paul. Sue thought this was a bad idea as most of the population were Muslims and they would not take kindly to a christian telling them who to believe in.

Arman pointed out he believed that was what Jesus had meant for him and why he was chosen. Sue didn't think it was a great idea and would go along with him. Arman didn't think this was a great idea, as there may be fighting, and Sue could get hurt. Besides, someone had to stay back to run the Monastery and look after Sarah. Since Sue was around, he would try to see as many villages as possible and would take only a hand full of men with him as not to attract attention. The rest he would leave to protect the Monastery. Sue argued with Arman, but could see she was getting nowhere, so she stopped and went to her own room to see what was on television.

CHAPTER 18

Arman drove into a small village and noticed there was a church on the outskirts. He drove up to it and could see that no one was inside, and the entrance was boarded up. He pulled the boards off and opened the church doors. It was obvious the church had not been used for some time and had been ransacked by the tribes in the area. Even the crucifixes had been pulled off the wall and smashed.

He had two of his men stay guard outside and went in to see what was inside. The pews were serviceable, but all other things would need to be cleaned, and the church swept before anyone could enter. As he was looking inside, several women came in from a side door to ask what he was doing. He explained he intended to open the church and carry out services for the Christians in the area. The women advised him that about fifty percent of the population were Christians, and the rest were Muslims.

The women told Arman that about two years ago, a tribal leader named Fadel Mansur stopped Christians from having services there. He shot their minister to ensure no one carried out any Christian services. They feared there would be trouble if he came back and found the church open.

Arman told the women that Fadel was dead and would not trouble them. Upon hearing this, the women were very keen to help Arman clean and open the church. They went to the bell tower and rang the bell. Shortly after, a group of twelve women arrived and eagerly volunteered to clean the church so that a service could take place.

The word spread that the church was opened, and a service would be held on Sunday.

The church was packed, and it was agreed that three services would be held on Sunday rather than just one. All would be handled by Arman.

Before the services started, two ministers who were hiding amongst the community came forward to assist Arman in holding the services.

That Sunday, Arman attend to the morning service and each of the other ministers held the other services. The ministers agreed to stay in their roles and would reach out to Arman if they need help or face any issues with the local tribes.

Arman's morning service started with prayer as usual. However, halfway through, he became suspicious of the bearded men wearing coats in the crowd, thinking they might be carrying weapons. He stopped the service and asked those present to take off their coats to ensure no one was carrying a weapon. Arman said, 'This is a sanctuary where men and women can give prayers to their God. Not a place where Muslim can show their hatred for Christians and kill in cold blood.'

The leader of the group immediately moved to the front and pulled out a rifle and aimed it at Arman, who expected this move and grabbed the rifle from his hand and hit him with the butt sending the tribesman in a free fall to the floor, unconscious.

The other tribesmen, seeing their leader being disarmed and unconscious, hastened to protect him and to move him to a safer environment. No one prevented them from picking him up and carrying him out. As soon as they left, Arman gave thanks to the Lord for protecting the congregation and allowing the service to continue. At the end of the service, Arman noticed some religious leaders at the back of the hall, carefully listening for any references to the Muslim faith. After the service ended, they moved to the front and approached Arman.

The senior cleric says, 'I see you are reopening the church and have held services.' Arman moved down to introduce himself. He then led the way to a room where they could sit and talk privately. Some refreshments were ordered, and the conversation began in earnest.

The senior cleric says, 'We understand you came close to being killed by the leader of one of the tribes. You disarmed him and knocked him out, preventing a blood bath taking place. Who are you, as no average person could have done what you did?'

Arman tells the clerics as to what had happened to him when he tried to lift the cross from its base and that he now is in the service of God spreading the word. His men were used to protect the church and the orphanage from tribesmen.

The clerics were happy that the church was reopened, but some people in the area still had extreme views and threatened the lives of Christians, like before.

Arman said, 'It is up to us to ensure both Christian and Muslim faith may exist side by side. To kill those who follow an alternative faith diminishes the society we live in.'

The men agreed to do their best to stop tribesmen from using weapons against another religion and to promote tolerance between their followers.

The meeting ended up with an invitation being given to Arman to join the clerics at the mosque next Sunday which Arman accepted.

Arman attended the mosque on Sunday but did not give his prayer to Allah, but instead to Jesus Christ. The clerics comprehended and refrained from making an issue of this.

With no threats, the two religions peacefully coexisted and brought temporary peace to the area. The warring tribes did not like it but would not disobey the clerics. If they wanted to kill each other, then that was their prerogative, but not unarmed innocent church goers nor their children.

Arman knew his time had arrived when he must go back to the Monastery and plan on his next trip. He wondered whether Sue was still there or had she had been recalled back to the studio to complete her film. He planned to leave on Sunday after his mass and would leave a few men behind to prevent attacks. As the region becomes safer, their numbers would slowly decrease.

Arman left his men with a truck and enough supplies and ammunitions to see them through a couple of months of holding the piece. The police re-established themselves in the township and law and order would come back to the community.

Arman began his long trip back to the Monastery and arrived after everyone had gone to bed. His men unpacked the firearms and decided to attend to the rest the next morning.

CHAPTER 19

The Monastery bell rang at five, and all woke to a new morning. They all assembled at the church for morning prayer before breakfast. As Sue walked in, she was surprised to see Arman, especially in one piece. She approached him and asked about his trip. However, the other sisters were also curious, so they decided to gather at midday for him to share his journey with everyone. After prayer, each would shower and then attend to breakfast. They would then prepare breakfast for the children at the orphanage. All children were then bathed and fed and allowed to play.

Everyone would then attend to their duties throughout the day and then would prepare for the evening routine.

Midday came and everyone assembled at the church. Arman stood up and went into the pulpit. He described the area they went in to, to spread the word and that they had found a christian church that had been boarded up for many years. The Muslims would attack the christians and the christians did likewise. There was no peace in that village.

Arman continues and says, 'We opened the church and began cleaning it out when some christians in the area came to help us prepare the church for service. The Muslim ministers came and advised us not to open the church as this would lead to attacks and the continual loss of life. We refused to listen to them and continued with our plans to open the church and spread the word of Jesus Christ.'

On the first day, there were more armed Muslims than Christians in the church. But we managed to disarm the leader and prevent any harm to ourselves. We met with Muslim clerics who agreed to help us establish the church and discourage their followers from attacking Christians. We stayed a week and left, leaving some men to ensure there were no attacks or to report back should trouble occur.

Arman said, 'I want to replicate what we have here, as I saw many children struggling to get food and shelter in that area. I assume they face the same challenges as the children here at the Monastery, where they are needlessly harmed or left to fend for themselves. I would like some sisters to join me on my next trip there to establish an orphanage and eventually replicate what we have here.'

Everyone was very excited to hear about the trip and that an orphanage and medical centre would be established at the new church to help the community. Three Sisters immediately stood up, volunteering to move to the new area and establish the facilities required. Arman advised he intended to revisit the area in about two weeks' time, and they were welcomed to join him. If they intend to make the move, they should pass on their duties at the Monastery as they wouldn't be returning for a while.

He also mentioned that to do this work would require more money than what they had raised for the Monastery. He hoped Sue would assist in again trying to raise the funds through appearances at talkback shows in America.

Sue was taken aback by Arman's comments, especially regarding using her to fundraise for the facilities. However, she acknowledged that her fame could help her gain access to affluent people.

Sue pointed out to Arman that she was needed on another set shortly to start a new movie and could not devote the time to being a fundraiser. Arman said, 'I know this, but you are recognised worldwide and out of all of us, the only one equipped to do this. None of the others have the expertise or talent to raise the funds. Sue had to agree and reluctantly accepted the task.

About a week passed when Sue received an invitation to appear on a talk back show in the States. As she had some commitments to attend to for her next movie, she agreed to appear. She wrapped up her work at the Monastery and, after saying goodbye to all, flew off to the States to fulfill her commitments.

Appearing at the show, she could discuss her up-and-coming movie, which would be screened throughout America in the coming weeks. The host then asked her what she did between movies, trying to embarrass her by having to admit she did nothing of relevance.

Sue guessed what the commentator was trying to do and said, 'Stange, you ask. I have been helping at the Monastery that was established some years ago and at the orphanage and medical centre.'

The commentator had forgotten about this and only remembered when Sue spoke about the Monastery.

Sue said, 'Now that you mention it, I might bring you up to date with what has been happening there. We set up an orphanage and medical centre at the Monastery. The American government acquired it and now gives an annual donation as part of their foreign aid. The establishment is not only a hospital but has become a school to train doctors within the area.' Sue received applause from the crowd as she explains their expansion into another area, which had many abandoned children and no medical facilities.

Sue continued and said, 'We are looking for donations to fund this establishment.' The commentator immediately interrupted and said, 'We do not have the structure to accept donations, and anyhow my understanding is that nothing comes from caring for the orphans, we really only give them food and board.'

With that, the crowd booed him, and a lady stood up and yells out, 'You don't know what you are saying. Look at these two children. My husband and I could not have a family because of how I was treated as a child by my father. These two children were officially adopted by us when they were less than a year old. They are our children now and we love them as if we gave birth to them.'

The commentator piped up and said, 'Yes, there is always one in the crowd which has benefited from the establishment of the orphanage.'

As soon as he said those words, four other ladies stood up and were very keen to show off their children, which they also adopt from the orphanage. The crowd was not on the side of the commentator and sensed he was trying to show that it was a waste of money to donate to the orphanage. The producer announced Red Cross is accepting donations on behalf of the charity and provided the bank account number for sending money. This was also scripted on the bottom of the screen to aid those who did not have a pen and paper ready to take the details.

Sue asked everyone to see what they could donate to help the children. The commentator tried to interrupt her and was forced to give in and allow the rest of the show to discuss the purpose of the funds and what would be needed. Newspapers heard about the success at the Monastery and published stories about it and the upcoming new establishment. Talkback radio stations also took up the story, and the donations came in.

Sue went to where the parents were that stood up with their children. She remembered two of the parents and the cameras were on her as she greeted the ladies and their children with kisses. This screened nationwide and added a human element to what was trying to be achieved. As part of the worldwide syndication, the show was screened to most countries, which helped more money being donated towards the charity. The American government agreed to assist by acquiring the church and creating an orphanage and hospital, just like it did at the Monastery.

By this time, the commentator had been humiliated and was very keen to bring the show to an end. Sue was very grateful to the Lord for giving her the opportunity to use her name to aid and support the charity and have an involvement in it. She remembered Mary, and how this all started and shed a tear as she pondered as to what the Monastery had become.

Unfortunately, she had committed herself to another movie and could not devote her time to the Monastery. This would be difficult as Sarah and Timothy got used to her being around daily. It would also break her heart not to see the children for a few months.

Sue remained in America for the next week, performing in shows and appearing on TV to discuss the charity's past accomplishments and plans. Once she had honoured all her commitments, she flew back to the Monastery and was warmly welcomed by the sisters and the children.

Sue reflected in her room on what had been accomplished and how the Lord had utilised her to establish the Monastery and grow her charitable work. She kneeled and prayed to God, asking for forgiveness and guidance in her life and relationship with Jesus Christ.

Sue went to the orphanage and noticed no one had taken Sarah out to be with the other children. She thought about it for a minute, then picked Sarah up and took her into the church. She put Sarah below the cross and knelt and prayed. As she praying the donkey came in and stood behind her and knelt. She thought this was odd but had seen it doing this before. As she was praying, she noticed Sarah moving in her blanket that was wrapped around her. She unwrapped the blanked to stop it constricting her and to give her some freedom.

Sarah moved around and threw the blanket off and tried to pull herself up. Sue got up just as the donkey moved forward towards Sarah.

Sue rushed towards Sarah to pick her up before she fell again, but Sarah didn't want to be held. She wanted to stand and walk. As soon as Sue picked Sarah up, she heard Arman say, 'The miracle has happened.' Sue turned to see Arman standing behind her with a booming smile on his face. Sue went to where Arman was standing and sat down in the pew.

Sue said, 'I can't understand it. Why now?

Arman said, 'You didn't believe in Jesus Christ, whereas now I think you do. It is your belief that saved Sarah.'

Sue says, 'But we both prayed, and nothing happened.'

Arman said, 'Yes, but before I was the only believer, the only one who had faith, whereas now you understand Jesus had been guiding your life since you were born and has used you for his work. You have achieved much for our charity and have used your image for the good of the charities to help other people and not just to enrich yourself.'

Sue sat with Arman while Sarah pulled herself up, only to fall again, but she would not give up. Sarah could now move and felt everything, including being able to bend and sit, whereas this was not possible before. Sarah crawled around and tried to get to her feet and with each movement, could do better than before.

A doctor was called in from the hospital who specialised as a paediatrician. He too had to declare it to be a miracle, as Sarah was previously restricted from the chest down and no one could have helped her overcome the damage done to her central nervous system.

After a while, the donkey decided he had enough of Sarah using him as a post to stand up and just turned and went back to the barn. Sue went to pick Sarah up, but she did not want to be carried. Eventually, she capitulated, and Sue took her to the playground so all the other children could see her.

Some Sisters were in church when the miracle happened and saw what transpired and could bear witness to what had occurred. While others learnt from the grapevine.

Timothy didn't know about Sarah, so it was a total surprise to him when she stood up and could move around like the other children except walk quickly, as children do. Sue sat there, allowing the children to play until it became time to prepare their dinner. She asked one sister to monitor her and went to assist in the kitchen.

The children were taken care of, bathed, fed, and put to bed. Following that, the staff could enjoy their meal. The main talking point at the table was the miracle that happened to Sarah and prayers were offered to the Lord by all that he had healed Sarah.

Sue saw the miracles that happened to Arman and Sarah, but she still wasn't sure about believing in God. She seemed to sit on the fence between believers and nonbelievers.

During dinner, one question cropped up, which worried Sue. That being now Sarah was healed, she most probably could be adopted out, possibly with Timothy. Sue couldn't stop thinking about this, as it was a possibility. She was a film star, not a mother, and the children need a home where they could grow up and be educated. Sue did not want to give up the children, as she had looked after them more than any other person.

Sue went to Arman to get an answer as to what she should do. Arman suggested finding a husband and getting married and have children of your own, which did not go down well with Sue. Arman did not believe Sue could adopt the children, as she could not give them a home. She was a film star moving around country to country, depending which country the film was being shot in. Not much of a life for the children. Also, if she established a base in America, she would not see the kids as she would be expected to be three to four months away from home filming. She did not want to give the children up, so she went to the adoption agency at the Monastery to discuss her adopting Sarah and Timothy.

The agency knew the children thought Sue to be their mother but believed that they most probably would forget Sue if they were adopted out soon.

The basic requirements were for the parents to be in a relationship or married and have a home to give stability to the life of the children. Sue did not meet this criterion but clarified that not all couples that adopt stay together. Marriages break up and couples cannot guarantee a stable family life. The agency agreed, but this is what they were looking for initially. Thereafter, it is not possible to predict what will happen over time.

Sue knew there would be many obstacles, but was willing to try, so she filled out the papers to get the process in motion and handed them to the agency.

CHAPTER 20

Sue sat in her office working away when Arman came in and sat down near her. He looked at her and could see she was stressed out.

Arman said, 'What is wrong? You look terrible, as if you haven't slept last night.'

Sue says, 'I am worrying about my application to adopt Timothy and Sarah. I got this feeling that they may not consider me to be an appropriate parent for the children.'

Arman said, 'Well, we should pray and asked the Lord's help. He will do what is best for them,'

Sue says, 'A lot a good that will do. We are relying on a man-made decision and not God's.'

Arman said, 'Yes, but God moves in mysterious ways, and he will decide what is best for all concerned.'

Sue says, 'I doubt it. I have the feeling things are going to go against me.'

Arman said, 'I thought you believe in God and your doubts are behind you?'

Sue says, 'I don't know. I just don't have the belief you have in God.'

Arman said, 'But I thought after the miracles that happen to me and Sarah, you totally believed in God. He showed you more than just a sign. You saw for yourself what he can do. In Sarah's case, no doctor could have cured her, yet God made her well.'

Sue says, 'Well, she was fixed. But how do I know it was God who did it? It could be the devil for all I know. I have never met God, so I wouldn't know what he looks like. I have never felt God and all my life he has stayed away from me, so I don't really know what to believe.'

Arman said, 'Sue, you look like one of those people who say, show me a sign and I will believe you, but they never do, even when a sign is given to them. Jesus Christ raised Lazaret from the dead, yet many who witnessed this still did not believe. He made the blind see yet again many who witnessed this still did not believe. Sue, do you believe in Jesus Christ?'

Sue considered the question and then said, 'I know what you are saying, but even though I saw what he did for you when you were ill and what He did for Sarah, I am still not sure he exists. I do not know how these things came about. He has done nothing for me. All I know is when I needed Jesus Christ, He was never there for me, and I believe He will not be there this time.'

Arman looked at Sue for a moment and then turned to go out of Sue's office. As he turned, Sue says, 'What have I said that makes you look at me that way? I have been honest with you.'

Arman said, 'It is not a sign that you are after, but something that I fear will register deeply with your soul and will cause you a lot of pain and anguish. It is an experience rather than a sign is what you're after. God showed you two miracles that could not have been performed by anyone else except Him and yet you require more to be convinced of His existence.'

Sue says, 'I am sorry to cast doubt on Him. It most probably is my mental state worrying I will not be able to adopt the kids. As soon as this is resolved, I will be able to think clearer and then possibly cast my doubts out the window.'

Arman said, 'I doubt that, Sue. I can only say that I am here if you need me, but I fear the Lord will drop you in a deep, deep hole and let you languish there until you have unequivocal faith in Him. You will be put in a position that no one on this earth will be able to help you out of, except God, and He will only help you if you firstly seek out Jesus Christ, his son. If it is an experience that you are after rather than a sign, then I am sure he will accommodate you.'

Arman then walked out of Sue's office and went into the church. He sat in a pew for a few minutes and then said a pray, 'Lord, I am lost for words as to Sue not having total and unequivocal faith in you. Thank you for the miracles you performed, especially in healing Sarah. I ask you do not punish Sue for her disbelief and ask you to help her find the path to you. I know the Holy Spirit indwells in those who believe in you and at present it has not been sent to Sue. Please protect her and guide her back to you and the path of righteousness. Amen.'

Chapter 21

Sue sat with Sarah and Timothy in the Manager's office who had the final say regards adoptions. After approximately ten minutes, he opened his door and requested that Sue come in without the children. He advised one of his staff will look after them while Sue was in his office.

Sue entered his office and sat down in the chair he directed her to take. She sensed things were not going to plan as everything was very formal with the necessity of every "i" dotted and "T" crossed.

The manager sat down and immediately advised Sue that he supported the recommendation to decline her the right to adopt the children. He advised Sue that a couple in the States have agreed to adopt both children and the agency have agreed to allow them the right to do so.

Sue was momentarily taken aback as to what the manager had just said and couldn't understand what he had said. She looked confused and angered by this decision and advised the manager to repeat what he had just said. He did this and Sue replies, 'That he was making a great mistake, as they have always seen her as their mother.' The Manager advised Sue that they have done preliminary checks on a young couple in the States, and they seem more suitable to adopt the children. He also advised Sue that one parent would arrive today to collect both children and take them back to the States.

Sue was beside herself and didn't know what to say or think. She was in a daze and switched off, not listening to the manager speaking. She couldn't think and only sat there, staring at the wall behind the manager.

The manager came up to Sue and tapped her on the shoulder, which seemed to bring her back to earth. He assisted her in getting up and cautioned her against seeing the children as they were being prepared to leave the orphanage.

Sue says, 'You can go to hell. I will speak to them and tell them what is happening.'

Manager says, 'No you will not be allowed as I understand they have been already collected and are on their way to the airport.'

Sue walked out of the office quickly and headed for Arman's office. Upon entering, she discovered he was not there. She walked to the church, and he was with a parishioner discussing a matter with them. She interrupts him and says, 'I have an urgent matter to discuss with you.'

Arman said, 'You will have to wait, Sue. I will be finished in about ten minutes.' Sue sat in a pew and waited. Arman finished with the couple he was talking to and then went to where Sue was sitting. He noticed she was in a hysterical state.

Hyperventilating and not her normal pleasant self. Arman said, 'Sue, what is the matter?'

Sue says, 'They have given Sarah and Timothy to another couple who have already collected the children and will take them back to the States. I will never see them again.'

Arman said, 'That was quick. I would have thought they would not have got the various reports back yet. Let's see what reports they have got back, and which ones are still outstanding.'

Arman and Sue went to the adoption manager's office to see what the police search report says about the couple adopting Sarah and Timothy.

The manager was absent, so the assistant didn't let them see the adoption file and application because of privacy rules. They left saying they would return.

Sue waited a couple of hours and again went to the adoption manager's office. This time he was in his office, but his assistant could not allow Sue to speak to him, as he had appointments for the rest of the day. She booked an appointment for two days later, at ten in the morning. Sue went back to Arman's office and advised him what she had done. Both Arman and Sue felt it was strange that the agency would not allow them to inspect the records, especially as both were part of the facility. It was agreed that they would again try to inspect the records after dinner.

The daily routine was followed in that Sue would help bath and feed the children before they could sit down and have their own meal. Sue felt bad when she was bathing the children, as she normally looked after Sarah and Timothy. She felt lost without them and became emotional and was told to snap out of it or leave it to the other sisters to handle. But Sue refused to and carried on without busting into tears or becoming emotional.

Once everyone had their meal and all was washed up and put away, Sue and Arman walked over to the adoption office and found the outer office was unlocked. They walked in and tried the manager's office, but it was locked. Sue had the master key, so she unlocked the door, and both walked in, and Sue switched the light on.

They found the cabinet, which contained the files on all the adoptions, and looked through it until they reached the one on Sarah and Timothy. They opened the file and read the application. To their horror, the children were adopted by two men. There was no police report in the file. No supporting documentation regards the character of the applicant. No indication of the type of work they did. Nothing supporting their financial details.

They looked at two more files and found that they were completed correctly. Each check had supporting documents, such as police reports on the applicants, employment and financial information, and character references from local ministers and community members. Why then did the file on Sarah and Timothy not contain these reports?

Arman put the files back, switched off the light, and left the office. Neither could understand why the file did not contain the required records and how the children could be adopted without these checks being done.

It was agreed that Arman would approach the adoption manager the next morning to see if he could have access to the file. If refused, he would insist on Interpol being brought in to investigate what had happened.

The next morning, Arman went to the adoption manager's office and was told he was not expected in until after lunchtime. He left and returned around two in the afternoon. The manager was in his office and was pleased to see Arman.

Arman asked for the file on Sarah and Timothy, but the manager refused to release it on privacy grounds. Arman pointed out as the senior officer in the establishment, he had the right to inspect all records and demanded the file be supplied to him. The manager got up and went to the main office and came back with the file. Arman then sat down in the manager's office and went through the file. He questioned the manager as to why the two men were allowed to adopt the children. The manager advised he did not make the decision and was unaware that they were two men rather than husband and wife. Arman asks, 'Where was the police check' and was told 'It should be in the file, otherwise it had been misfiled.'

Arman raised the issue as to where were the character checks and was told they should be in the file, otherwise they could be misfiled.

The missing documents were requested by Arman to be found, and the search was to be done immediately. He requested the manager contact him as soon as the records were located.

The manager agreed. Arman then left the office, closing the file and handing it back to the manager.

He went to his office and emailed a relative in America, asking for his help to track down the whereabouts of the two men who were allowed to adopt the children. He told his friend that these men had adopted two young children without providing police records or character references, which made the whole thing seem suspicious.

The next day, Arman's FBI agent friend told him that one man had a long criminal history, and the other had just been released from prison after being convicted of pornography. Both were selling pornography on the black market and were backed up by criminals with an international network.

Arman went to Sue's office and advised her of what he found out. Sue was very concerned and asked Arman to see if his friend could go to the premises shown to see if the kids were there and to take them away. Arman emailed the request and shortly received an email advising the address was not legitimate and the whereabouts of the children unknown.

Arman and Sue went to the adoption manager's office, but he was not in. The staff could not say where he was. They checked his diary and found out that he had several appointments that day, but he had phoned the clients and cancelled the appointments. Arman notified his friend, who immediately notified Interpol. He informed the local authorities, who thought it was unlikely for the men to have got passports for the children or added them to their own passports in such a short time. They most probably would kill the children and hide out until they could get out of the country once they knew the authorities were after them.

It was decided not to broadcast the description of the children but to wait and see if they will try to fly out of the country to a safe haven. Otherwise, the children would be at risk.

The FBI sent two skilled investigators to assist local authorities. They arrived a day later and were immediately briefed as to what the local police knew, which was not much. It was established that the adoption manager, who had been in the position for about a year, was being paid off by the criminals to supply very young children to parents that were going to adopt them. The parents could get passports for the children and mostly came from America. Once they flew to America, the children would be forcefully taken from the parents and initially used in a phonography racket. Once they had a lot of exposure, the children would be sold to the highest bidder, who would then use them as sex slaves. As they were never registered in the country they were sent to, they just disappeared after a few years. The buyer could do anything he wanted with them, and most did. Eventually, the child would be killed and disposed of, with no one worrying as to what had happened to them. The process would then be repeated.

The investigators followed whatever lead came as they knew this was being run by a large organisation and many well-known people would be implicated.

CHAPTER 22

Sue sat at her desk wondering what she should do. Her manager wanted her to start a new film, but her heart was not in it. She was scared that they would find Sarah and Timothy and she would not be there for them.

The day dragged on, and Sue attended to her role as administrator of the Monastery. Arman had left to go to preach in another region, leaving her and Nicholas to handle all the problems back home.

At about eleven that morning, the police rang and asked if she could do an identification on a body they found in an alleyway. It was a male who had been shot through the head gangland style. The police asked Sue to identify the body. They suspected it was the adoption manager at the Monastery who gave the children to the man for illegal purposes. As he had no known relatives, Sue was asked to do the identification.

About half an hour later, the police came to Sue's office. They showed Sue some photographs of the body and the face of the man. Sue could identify the dead person as the manager in charge of adoptions. Some of the staff were also asked to come to Sues office, and they also identified the person as being the manager.

The police informed Sue that they investigated the manager's bank records. It was found out that he received twenty thousand dollars for each child he placed for adoption with a gang member involved in pornography and later sold as a sex slave. He had been involved in this activity for many years and was found out in his previous place of employment, which is why he was forced to leave them. He had sent dozens of children to the criminal organisation that were later sold to predators worldwide. Of these, two had been reported as demised. The rest have never been heard of.

The police left Sue to continue with their investigation. Sue went back to her desk and attended to the work that was mounting up.

Sue received a message from Arman that he had arrived at his destination and was setting up a church in the town centre to preach to the community. He had experienced no opposition yet to his intention to preach the word of Jesus Christ.

Sue pondered on her situation, not knowing what to do. Should she continue acting or give acting away and concentrate on her administrative work? She decided not to decide until she knew what the situation was with Sarah and Timothy.

Chapter 23

Arman knew it would not be easy to preach the word of God to a community that was predominately Muslims. Yet that was what he was asked to do. He looked around to see if there were any christian churches in the region but could not find any. He approached several people who advised him that there was a christian church in town, but this was demolished many years ago by the order of the Muslim Cleric. The church was burnt and then levelled, and all the ministers were killed. Since then, no one had preached the christian faith.

Arman couldn't find a church, so he located a large building and set it up as a church. Chairs were used instead of pews, and a makeshift cross stood at the front. A further cross was nailed to the outside of the building so all could see that this was a place of worship. Arman then waited.

No one came to enquire as to when a service was to be held, nor did anyone take interest as to who was the minister.

Arman saw no one walking past the building, so he went down the street to check if something was blocking the way.

He couldn't see any but noticed that there was a group of men standing at both ends of the street preventing people from passing the church.

People would walk down the street only to be intercepted by these men, ordering them not to walk that way and to avoid going down the street. Otherwise, they would end up with a bullet or being bashed.

Arman walked up to the two that were preventing patrons from walking down the street. One of them grabbed Arman as if he was going to hit him midsection. Arman turned the man around and hit him in the gut, causing him to lean over. As he did this, he hit him in the head and the man fell to the ground. The second tribesman ran up to assist his friend and took a swing at Arman. With that, Arman hit him in the face and a second blow to the other side of his head and the man fell to the ground alongside his friend.

Arman signalled to one of his men to give him a hand and both lifted the unconscious men into a utility parked alongside of the road. They kept the weapons just in case they were needed in the future. As they stood there, the owner of the utility came out of a house and moved to the driver's seat. He started the utility up and drove off with the two unconscious men in the back.

Arman then walked back to the church and put the guns and ammunition away. He went up the road again just to see if the other side was also being controlled. As he neared the intersection, two men grabbed him and wanted to know what he was doing and why wasn't he stopped by the men controlling the street at the other end. Arman replies, 'What men? There was no one up the street.' They looked at Arman and looked to see if anyone was controlling the other end. As they loosen their grip on Arman, he turned around and hit one of them in the face, sending him to the ground and he grabbed the other in a headlock and squeezed until he lost consciousness. Arman dragged the men behind some bushes and tied their hands behind their back and stuffed their scarfs in their mouths to stop them from screaming. He then took their weapons back to the church and hid them with the other ones he gained. He told his men to take care of them.

They loaded the two into their utility and drove off, intending to drive some miles out before dumping them. They drove through some areas in which no one lived. The roads resembled dirt tracks rather than highways. After driving for an hour, they pulled over and lifted the men out of the utility. As they lifted the first man out, he head butted the man closes to him sending him to the ground. The other man grabbed his rifle and shot the man in the head, killing him outright. The second man made a shoulder charge at the man with the rifle but was not quick enough. Arman's man hit him with the butt of his rifle and shot him as he fell to the ground.

The two dead men were dragged behind a small earth mount and left there for the foxes to feed on. The men then got back into the utility and drove back to the church. When they entered the church, they were surprised to see it half full of people waiting for the service to begin. Many said they did not come initially because they feared they would be shot, and the church burnt to the ground as had been done previously.

Arman began the service and noted halfway through it that there were four tribesmen at the back of the church. He continued and completed the service. Once everyone had left the hall, he approached the four sitting at the back of the church and asked if they were there for worship. One man replied, saying they were there to kick him out and set the place on fire.

Arman said, 'Why would you not allow the church to establish the christian faith?'

Tribesman says, 'We are Muslims and only the Muslim faith can be preached in this region.'

Arman said, 'Why there are christians here? Why not allow them to pray to their god?'

Tribesman says, 'Our cleric only allows the Muslim faith to be followed, and we have been ordered to kill anyone who declares themselves a christian.'

Arman warned that if the Cleric didn't change the order by midnight, all Clerics and their followers who held that belief would die without seeing the sunrise.

Tribesman says, 'And how are you going to kill all of us? You most probably have a dozen men with you, whereas we have villages in this region with a lot of fighting men. We have at least five hundred men close by. You could not make it to the front door of the mosque, let alone trying to get close enough to the clerics to kill them.'

Arman said, 'Then you will see. Our God has spoken. If your clerics refuse to allow christians to pray to their God, then they will not see tomorrow's sunrise.'

With that, the tribesman got up and walked out to convey the message to the Clerics. They drove to the main mosque and stormed into the senior Cleric's office, who was surprised to see them back so soon.

Senior Cleric says, 'That was quick. What did you do with them? Shoot all of them?'

Tribesman says, 'No, we did nothing to them. We threatened them and said we most probably will kill them, but the minister told us to convey a message to you that all those who are objecting to their religion being practiced will at midnight be struck down and will lose their life. We said how are you going to do this, but they would not reply other than to say all those refusing to allow the christian faith to be preached and followed will die at midnight.'

The Senior Cleric says, 'Double your guards to ensure they do not attack us tonight. They must have a plan to hit us at midnight when we are all asleep. Send your men out to see where they are holding their tanks and rocket launches. They will need at least a thousand men, so see if you can find where they are being housed so we can hit them first. Such a concentration of equipment and men should be obvious. Go to find them and report back within the hour.'

They all disbursed to see what they could find.

One hour later, the tribesmen gathered in the senior clericals office and reported they could find nothing. No men, no equipment.

Senior cleric says, 'You should have shot them then and there. It would have put an end to all this rubbish. We will play their game and wait till midnight and then, after midnight, you are to bomb them out of existence and make sure you kill every one of them.'

The tribesman in charge sat down and looked at the clock. He ordered his next in command to prepare the men as they were going to destroy the church and kill all the christians.

Mid night arrived, and the clock chimed twelve. As the last stroke of the clock bellowed out, all in the room died. No one was left alive. All in the main mosques who were on their knees praying fell to the floor and died.

The next morning, Arman woke up and prepared himself for the morning service. Parishioners came in and were talking about the number of bodies they noticed in the streets and that all in a mosque had died that night.

Arman began his service, but the noise of vehicles on the street interrupted him. These vehicles were carrying bodies to be buried in a mass grave outside the township, following the Muslim custom of burial within 24 hours of death.

The mass concluded, and all went back to their homes fearing that if they stayed, they would be attacked by the Muslims. Arman took a stroll to see what had happened. There were bodies in the streets. He spoke to one man and found out that nearly all the clerics and half of the tribesmen died that night. Too many to be individually buried, so a mass grave was being prepared and all would be buried that day.

The christian religion was left to carry on and was never again challenged in that region.

After a few days, Arman was approached by two men who introduced themselves as ministers of the former church. They were acting underground to ensure they were not found out and killed. They requested to be allowed to continue as ministers and took over from Arman.

Arman left them in the town and prepared to go back to the Monastery. He stayed a further week and then he and his men made their way back to the Monastery, leaving three men to protect the ministers should there be trouble.

Chapter 24

Sue finally interviewed all those who had applied to become head of the adoption office. Police checks had been done on all applicants and all showed up negatively, with no involvement in the underworld.

Out of the applicants, Sue chose two who she felt could handle the job and passed their names on to Arman for his final selection.

Sue sat there while the sisters discussed the applicants and how to protect the children from being sold or exploited.

The conversation got intense as some sisters insisted that the adoption manager should be a team of two people, both of whom had to sign off before giving a child to a prospective parent. During the conversation, the phone rang, and Sue picked up the call.

Sue says, 'Sue speaking.'

Caller says, 'My name is Sargeant Morris. We have received a tipoff as to where the two missing children are and need someone to make an identification.'

Sue says, 'Can you being them here at the Monastery so I and the sisters can identify them?'

The room became quiet, and all were trying intensely to listen in to the conversation.

Caller says, 'No we cannot do that as the children are demised and their bodies burnt.'

Sue upon hearing that the children were dead screamed out, 'O God no they were only babies, and you allowed this to happen to them.' She became hysterical bursting into tears and screaming out, 'Not my babies.' She then fell to the floor hitting the arm of the chair as she went down.

As she fell out of her chair, some sisters got up and moved towards her, trying to stop her from falling to the floor.

One Sister then took the phone and said, 'My name is Sister Adrian. Can you please repeat what you just said to Sue? She has fainted and currently we are trying to get her to come around with smelling salts.'

Caller repeated who he was and what he had said to Sue.

Sister Adrian says to the other sisters, 'They have located two bodies that could be Sarah and Timothy. Both have been killed and their bodies burnt. The police want us to go down to identifier them as they believe they are the missing children. They will send a police car to pick us up and take us to the morgue. I will go with Sister Reilly. Take Sue to the clinic and have them check her out and monitor her condition.'

With that, the two sisters went to their rooms to wait for the police car to arrive. Sue was taken to the clinic, and they gave her a sedative to calm her down.

Arman was notified as to what had happened, and he agreed to accompany the sisters to the morgue.

The police car arrived within ten minutes of the call, and all were transported to the morgue.

Seargent says, 'I must warn you the bodies are in a terrible state, and you may not be able to identify them. Do your best, but if you are overcome by grief, then turn and walk away. We understand.'

The morgue operator then opened a door and pulled out a long table to reveal a child's body, which was partially burnt.

The Sisters, seeing the body, drew back at the horrible sight before them. Some put their hands over their faces to stop them from vomiting.

Sister Adrian says, 'Who would do this to a baby? Yes, the body appears to be that of Sarahs.'

Sister Reilly says, 'I cannot tell you whether it is or isn't Sarah. The body's size matches Sarah's, but her face is unrecognizable because of severe fractures caused by a powerful blow.'

The morgue attendant says, 'The autopsy revealed she had been rapped, repeatedly after her death.'

Arman then stepped forward and stared at the body, thinking to himself, 'Which animal would do this to a child of three?'

He looked at the body for a moment and says, 'I am not sure, but I would be more likely to say it is Sarah rather than say it wasn't her. The fact that we cannot tell from the facials makes this hard, but the rest seems to be the same size.' Arman was not overcome by seeing the condition of the body, because he had seen burnt bodies before when he led his tribe in raids and set fire to villages. He then stepped back, and the attendant covered the body with the white sheet and pushed the table back into the cabinet and closed the outer door.

The technician then opened another door and pulled out another tray containing the body of another child. He removed the sheet to reveal a young male child with facial damage again, as if being hit in the face and head by a forceful object like a fist or hammer. The body also showed scaring and blue marks to the buttocks area.

The attendant says, 'the autopsy revealed that the child was punched several times and forceful raped before death.'

Arman, after looking at the body, said, 'I couldn't say either way if this was Timothy. Look at the body. Some animal has inflicted a lot of pain on this child before he died. It was difficult to see his appearance because of the burns, making it impossible to confirm if the body was Timothy's. He then stepped aside for Sisters Adrian and Reilly to identify it. Both Sisters looked at the horrible sight but could not declare this to be Timothy.

The morgue attendant then covered up the body and pushed the table in and closed the door. The policemen standing near them said, 'We will show you have identified the first body to be that of Sarah's and the second body, possibly that of Timothy.

Everyone agreed, and they then went off and were driven back to the Monastery.

Back at the Monastery, they made their way to Sue's office where she was siting staring at the back wall. They walked in and sat down. She didn't notice them coming in until Arman yells out 'Sue' and she looked up, startled from her gaze.

They told Sue that they could not positively identify the bodies belonging to Sarah and Timothy and described them to her. She was visibly shaken to hear the babies were subjected to rape and torture and were physically punished and beaten to death. Sue was crying as they described what they saw and what they believe happened to the children.

While Arman and the two sisters were at the morgue, Sue's manager called and told her they needed her on the set within two weeks. They also said they would arrange for her to pick up her ticket at the airport. Sue was unsure about going because she didn't want to be there if Sarah and Timothy were found. But now that they had been identified, there was no reason for her to stay at the Monastery, as it would always remind her of them. Sue thought it would be good for her to change her surroundings, so she told everyone she'd be leaving in a week to finish her contract.

Everyone believed this was the wrong decision and recommended she delay the film for a month so she could recover mentally from the death of Sarah and Timothy. But Sue thought a change in scenery was the best way for her to stop thinking about the children and what had happened to them.

She decided to leave as she had planned. They all broke up and left Sue to think about what had been said to her.

The morgue released the bodies to Arman, who attended to the burial arrangement. All the sisters and half of the medical staff attended. Sue was there but was not a speaker. It was a sombre affair, with most naming the death of the children a tragedy and God would punish those involved. At the end of the service, all were asked to pass by the caskets and place a rose on top or nearby, which most did. Sue was in tears as she passed Sarah's casket and stood there a moment, crossed and moved on. She went back to her seat and at the end went to her room in tears to pack her belongings as she was due to fly out the next day.

No one was much in the mood to have dinner, nor to speak of the children or the funeral. All were upset as to what had happened to the children and the tremendous suffering they would have gone through at the hands of their assailants. All it seems went to bed early to ponder on the day's events and the tremendous suffering the children would have gone through.

Sue had little sleep that night. She kept waking up and thinking about the children and what she should have done to ensure she adopted them. She should have moved earlier and if she did, they would still be alive. For them, she should have given away her movie career.

After showering, getting dressed, and packing the last items in her bag, she went downstairs to get breakfast. She helped herself and sat down, only to be joined by Arman. They both had their breakfast and then broke up to do the last things before heading to the airport.

They met outside, and all were there to say goodbye again to Sue. She hugged and kissed all the sisters, who insisted she kept in touch and come back soon. Arman took Sue's bags and loaded up in the car and after the last goodbyes, they headed for the airport.

At the airport, Arman could not accompany Sue to her departure lounge, as the parking was restricted, and it seemed that everyone was flying out at the same time. He loaded up a trolly with Sues bags. They both hugged each other, and Arman gave Sue a big kiss, asked her to ring him when she arrived, and then got in his car and drove off. Sue was surprised and momentarily stood there thinking what was that all about.

Sue gained her composure and pushed her trolly into the airport and headed for the departure lounge. After checking in her bags, Sue went to the departure lounge to wait on instructions to board the plane. After waiting an hour, she boarded her plane and, after a ten-hour flight, landed at her destination. She headed for her unit, which the studio had got for her and all the other actors in the film.

Sue booked herself in and went to her room to get some rest, as she could not sleep on the plane. She ordered a small meal which was delivered to her room. She ate it all and then went to bed hoping to have got over her "jet lag" by the next day.

CHAPTER 25

Arman assembled his men and headed off to the eastern region. He was told there was a big Christian community there, but the ministers were deceiving the parishioners about what the bible said. They altered the words and claimed that the Bible's true meaning is wrong, promoting their own interpretation that didn't align with God's.

Arman drove for about twelve hours and had to make two stops before arriving at one village. He camped out on the outskirts of the town and drove in with two of his guards. All were casually dressed and therefore would not be recognised immediately as outsiders.

They arrived on a Sunday. They drove up the main street of the town and at the end of the street found what appeared to be a christian church. Arman noted a service was at ten o'clock, so he parked his car and, with his men, walked to the church. He told his men not to sit together but rather, spread themselves amongst the parishioners so as not to be noticed as coming from outside of town.

Parishioners had already assembled outside the church, waiting for it to be opened. He waited and ten minutes later, the church doors were opened, and the parishioners moved to their seats. Arman sat in the second pew from the front. Twenty minutes later, the service began. Arman noticed that the usual hymns were not sung before or after the main speech by the minister. Nor were there bible readings. The minister never referred to God or Jesus Christ, but continually referred to the State and what it was doing to bring Christianity into the modern era.

After forty minutes, the minister spoke to the congregation about accepting the state's decision on same-sex marriage and euthanasia. He tried to say that the bible declared parishioner should accept same-sex marriages, and quoted from Isaia saying this was stated in the Old Testament. With that, Arman stood up and moved to the pulpit. He grabbed the minister and threw him out of the pulpit with such force that he landed on the floor face down.

Arman said, 'Your minister is an antichrist. He is not preaching from the bible but making up most of what he says as he goes along. He, in fact, has misrepresented the bible and the word of God. Being a Charlot, he should not be allowed to be a minister. He is trying to get you to accept what the State wants you to do and not what the bible tells you. The bible is the word of God. The State is trying to get rid of God's word and take its place and this wolf in sheep's clothing is doing his best to have this happen.

Standing up, the minister made his way back towards the pulpit. He attempted to punch Arman, but Arman saw it coming and retaliated, knocking the minister to the ground. The bible does not accept same-sex marriages. A marriage is between a man and a woman, not between two men or two women, which are relationships, not marriages. To say or teach otherwise is contrary to the bible. The teaching of a marriage between two men or two women is a concept of the State and is based on legislation, not on religion. Therefore, the State wants to do away with the bible and religion and try to get what it wants to replace the bible. The wealthy who run government want to control your religion and if allowed, the word of God will be eliminated.

God will not allow this to happen. The State has its place, and so does the church. The State should not be allowed to control your beliefs nor dictate what is the word of God.

To allow euthanasia is contrary to the teaching of the bible. God created mankind. You had no say when you were going to be borne. It was God who delivered you into this world. You had no say in it, nor did you select the time or date of your birth. God did this. You were put on this planet to serve God, not yourself. To say you have the right to decide when you are departing is to say you do not believe in God as you do not trust him to bring you back home at the right time. You want to take matters into your own hands as you are your own God, and you think you know best. What you are setting yourself up for is a thousand years in hell, not a peaceful departure from this world. Yes, the death of your body will happen as it decomposes, but your soul will linger on in hell for a thousand years.

Arman noted some men had entered the church with guns. It seems the minister had men he could call upon to exert his mandate.

Arman advised the parishioner that the service was over, and it would be to their advantage to leave the church. With that, most moved out of the church, fearing retribution. All that was left were Arman's men dressed up as parishioner and the gunman. The leader moved up to Arman and ordered him from the pulpit. Arman stayed, to the annoyance of the man in charge. He moved up to the pulpit and tried to hit Arman in the head with his rifle. Arman expected this and moved out of his way and withdrew a pistol from the man's belt and shot the leader in the head. He fell to the ground. His men did not know what to do. Arman's men withdrew their weapons and aimed them at the men, ready to shoot. As the men raised their guns at Arman's men, they were fired upon, with all being killed. Arman prayed for forgiveness, but not to retaliate would have to allow the evil forces to take control.

He went outside to see if there were any more gunmen. He noticed there was a group of them at the end of the street, consisting of four men. There is no doubt they heard gunfire and must have assumed their team were the ones shooting and would have killed all that opposed the antichrist.

Arman decided to lure the men in and overcome them, if possible. Otherwise, they will have to shoot them. At that time, the previous minister entered the church thinking that Arman and his men had been killed. To his surprise, that was not the case, and Arman's men quickly surrounded him and made him sit in a pew until Arman returned. Two men were left to guard him while the other men went outside to see what was happening. Arman ordered them back into the church, as he did not want the other tribesmen seeing his men.

The minister tried to reason with Arman's men, even offering cash bribes which would never be paid. It was obvious the devil had entered the minister's body as his promises became more extravagant as time went on. Arman's men stepped away to talk about the offers, but then the minister unexpectedly pulled out a gun from under his robes and started shooting at them. He hit one of them in the heart, killing him outright and wounding the second. A guard at the back of the church, seeing what was happening, shot the minister in the head, killing him.

The guards from up the street, hearing the gunfire, walked down the street to investigate what had happened. As they approached the church, Arman ordered they put their weapons down. Instead of following his orders, they raised their guns and shot in the Arman's direction, who was behind a pillar. Their bullets hit the pillar. The return fire saw them killed where they stood. They had six men now dead, with no knowledge of where they could be taken. Arman noticed a truck parked up the road where the men were stationed at the head of the street. He went to investigate it and climbed into the cabin, noticing there was ammunition in the back and a few extra rifles.

He started the truck and drove it into the church's driveway. Removing the ammunition from the truck, he proceeded to load up the dead bodies. He drove the truck out of town and into an open space. Two cans of petrol were at the back of the truck. The petrol was tipped over the bodies and the inside of the cabin of the truck. He ripped a piece of cloth from the minister's robe, tied a rock to it and drenched it in petrol. He ignited the rag and threw it at the truck, setting it alight. It burst into a ball of flames, burning the truck, leaving a twisted chase.

As the truck burst into flames, Arman walked back to the church. He didn't want to be caught in the open, as no doubt they would associate him with the destruction of the truck. He walked behind the bushes so he could not be seen. Eventually, he got back to the church and explored what was there in the way of facilities. He was surprised to see there were accommodation for three individuals, a garage for four cars, and three classrooms to teach children. There was also what seemed to be a child-minding room or a preschool which had photographic equipment in it for videos and still pictures. It was clear that the minister was not alone in his enterprise. But where were the other ministers? Arman waited to see what would happen as the week progressed. He moved into what appeared to be the minister's quarters and would claim he was filling in for the minister while he took a break. His men were to take up the other two quarters temporarily.

CHAPTER 26

Sue was on the set, being directed as to how she was to play her part. She went through her lines with her co-actors. The director was happy with what he saw, so he declared the next take would be canned. Everyone got ready, and the Director yells out 'Action', and the team went into action until the end and the director yells out 'Cut'. Everyone was glad that the scene went off with no retakes.

Sue prepared herself for the next take and sat down to study her lines. Other actors came around her to discuss how they intend to do their scene. Each readout their lines and it was soon that the director yelled out for all to return on the scene.

The actors performed their lines and actions, and the director gave feedback and suggestions on how to improve. When the director was satisfied that everyone knew what he wanted, he called 'Action' and the film crew began filming the scene as played out. After about fifteen minutes, the director called 'Cut' and everyone was pleased to see the scene was shot successfully.

They all went through their lines for the next scene and again, when the director was happy with what he saw, he would call for the filming of the scene.

As the film progressed towards the evening, one actor's two children and his wife were brought on the scene to see their father working. The children were fascinated by the equipment and the hive of activity.

Sue was studying her lines when she looked up and saw a boy and girl looking at her. She stared back and then said, 'Sarah, is that you?'. The girl stopped in her tracks, not knowing what to say, other than to yell out the word 'Mummy.'

The girl's mother came up to her and took her by the hand, but the girl refused to go with her. Sue again looked at the girl and got up and walked to where she was standing. She says, 'Sarah, is that you?'. The girl's mother, who could see there was something wrong, bent down to pick up the girl when Sue says, 'Why are you taking my Sarah away?'.

The girl's mother quickly picked up the girl and hurried her away to where her husband was seated. She said, 'One of your co-workers has mistaken our daughter for someone called Sarah. The actor realised who his wife was referring to and went to Sue asking if she was alright.

Sue replies, 'No, I saw Sarah and I don't know where she has gone.' The actor tried to explain to Sue that it was his daughter who she saw and not Sarah, but Sue would not accept what was being said to her to the extent that she worked herself up into an anxious state and the paramedics had to be called.

The ambulance arrived within ten minutes of receiving the call and noticed Sue was in a poor mental state, not comprehending what was being said to her. They decided to take her to the hospital before she had a nervous breakdown.

Sue was examined by the doctors, who called in a psychiatrist to check her out. She was immediately put on a tranquilliser to calm her down. Sue could not comprehend what was being said to her and kept looking around for Sarah. Her mind was locked on seeing Sarah, who didn't exist. The doctors determined she couldn't go home and needed to stay in the hospital for a few days to understand her thoughts better.

Sue was placed in a private room and examined by two doctors, who agreed that she needed medication to calm her down and treat her hallucinations. She was placed on a course of tablets and checked daily by the doctors.

The doctors determined the drugs weren't working for her, so they prescribed different ones. However, nothing seemed to work, and Sue got worst in that she could not comprehend what was being said to her, nor could she concentrate on what she was saying. This went on for two more weeks. The doctors changed her tablets to ones that were recommended for her condition, to calm her down. These drugs unfortunately had side effects which caused depression and hallucination.

Sue began to see strange creatures that would fly around her room and perch on the end of her bed and talk to her. Sue would often see dwarfs chasing flying creatures in her room.

She would shut her eyes to avoid witnessing what happened when they caught one.

After a while, all would disappear, and Sue would be left looking into a black hole of depression. She would stare into the hole for hours without blinking. This would be repeated day after day, driving her mad.

One day, she decided it was not worth continuing with her life and to end it.

The next morning when the staff were changing the sheets on her bed, she took a pair of sheets off the trolly that was left outside of her room unattended.

Sue waited until that evening when there were less staff on the wards. She took the sheets to a storeroom which had two beams across the walls. She tied the sheets together and with the support of a long handle broom was able to loop the sheets across the beam and tied one end, so it held over the beam. With the other end, she tied it around her neck and stood on a large drum of cleaning fluid that was in the room. She thought to herself the words Jesus says when he died on the cross, 'It is finished' and then jumped off the drum.

The sheet tightened around her throat, and she began swaying as she grasped for air, thinking maybe this wasn't a good idea. She tried to move her legs and feet and tried to lessen the constriction of the sheets around her throat. As she gasped for air, she accidentally kicking the drum of cleaning fluid, tipping it over and sending it flying towards the wall with a thump. She pulled on the sheet once more, causing the knot to come undone and her body to fall to the floor, making a loud noise and hitting objects nearby.

As Sue fell, two nurses were walking past the room and heard the racket and walked in to see what was happening. They could immediately see what Sue was doing and called for doctors to assist.

The ward doctor came immediately and could see what Sue was trying to do. He took the sheets from Sue and escorted her back to her room and put her to bed, tying restraints on her to stop her from getting out of bed.

After fifteen minutes, Sue's psychiatrist arrived and asked her why she had attempted to take her own life. She couldn't understand his question and therefore couldn't answer and could only look bewildered as to what was being said to her.

It was apparent that she could not be treated with medication and that some other course of treatment would have to be considered.

Her doctor decided she should have a course of shock treatment to get her mind back to reality. The director of the film production was asked to come in and speak to the doctor, which he did. He could not provide much information as to Sue's next of kin other than to say she spent a lot of time at the Monastery, and they should make enquiries there. The doctor advised him that Sue may not be fit to resume her role in the movie, which would mean they would have to seek a new leading star for that role.

The hospital contacted the Monastery and eventually got onto Arman. He was deeply concerned to hear about Sue's nervous breakdown and her attempt to kill herself. After the call, he went and told the sisters who were also concerned. Those who knew Sue thought it would be best to bring her back to the Monastery. The hospital there could take care of her while her friends visited her and help her remember things.

Arman and the sister decided to fly over and see if they could help Sue. Within a day, after packing their bags for a four-day stay, they were heading off to the hospital to see Sue. They booked into a hotel close to the hospital and made their way to the hospital. They had an appointment with Sue's doctor, which they kept.

Her doctor explained that Sue still believed that Sarah was alive and would not accept she had died. She believed that someone had taken Sarah from her. What, in fact, she saw was a girl, which her mind kept telling her was Sarah.

Her doctor wanted to give Sue a course of shock treatment, which should jolt her mind back to reality. However, sometimes this type of treatment did not go according to plan, and the person got worst and not better. The doctor explained shock treatments could lead to memory loss, causing the person to forget their identity and origin. Their memory would normally come back to them within a month, but not always. There are risks involved, and that's why they seek permission from a next of kin.

Arman pointed out that there was no next of kin and they were only friends of Sue and not relatives and, as such, could not give permission.

Arman and the sister then went to see Sue, who didn't remember any of them. She looked bewildered when they said they were friends of hers. They stayed a while and then went back to their hotel and intending to revisit Sue in the afternoon.

Arman and the sister went back to the hotel to freshen up and to get something to eat. They relaxed until the evening and then went back to see Sue, who was sitting up in a chair, staring at the television. Sue didn't move or turn to see who had come into her room. She was in her own world and not conscious as to what was happening around her.

Arman and the sister sat there for an hour trying to start a conversation with Sue. Sue kept staring at the television, which was not on, not recognising anything around her and not responding to anything being said. The doctors informed Arman that they planned to use shock treatment on Sue to kick start her mind.

Since there was no known next of kin, the doctors planned to start the first treatment the following day. They hoped Arman would stay until it was completed, as Sue might regain her memory after the first treatment.

Arman and the sister agreed to stay an extra day and made plans to come back the next morning. They got up and walked out with the doctors, leaving Sue alone, staring at the blank television.

The next day, Arman and the sister arrived at the hospital and went to Sue's room. She was again siting in her chair staring at the back wall, not noticing what was going around her. They sat close to Sue, who did not move or blink. She just starred at the wall. The doctors came in and placed Sue in a wheelchair and took her off to the medical lab where the shock treatment was going to be performed. Arman and the sister were allowed to follow and witness the procedure.

Sue was put in a chair, and her arms tied down on the leather armrests. A metal ring was lowered down and tightened on her forehead. All the doctors then moved back into a room nearby which had computer screens displaying Sue from all directions. The process entailed sending an electric current to the unit fastened to Sue's head, with the tensity being increased over time.

The doctors started the unit up and send a mild current to Sue's head. She moved as the current hit her. The doctors increased the voltage at the level they thought was right for Sue and allowed her to stay at that level for about three minutes. They then decreased the current until the unit came to a stop.

Sue was unconscious. The doctors removed her arm restraints and the metal ring from her forehead. They put her in a wheelchair and took her back to her room. Arman and the sister went with them and stayed there for a while to see if Sue regained consciousness and recognised them. They sat there for two hours while Sue slept. Since she was not showing any sign of waking, they decided to go back to the hotel and pack for their departure the next day.

Sue slept through the day and night and woke the next morning, not knowing where she was. She tried to get out of bed but was restrained by several belts tied around her waist and the sides of her bed were up, preventing her from getting out of bed. Eventually, a nurse arrived and buzzed for a doctor.

The doctor ordered Sue to be allowed out of bed and allowed her to walk around. Sue remembered nothing and looked at the doctor and nurse as to say, 'Who the hell are you?'

The doctor explained to Sue she had shock treatment, which would leave her with memory loss. All should come back to her within a day or two, and not to worry about the lack of knowing where she was and how she came to be where she was. They sat Sue down and got a new gown for her and the nurse took her to the shower and let her shower herself. Sue had her shower and put on the hospital gown, as she did not have any of her own clothes. She had her breakfast and sat in the chair thinking who was she and what was she doing in the hospital. Arman and Sister Rachel came in, and Sue stared at them as if she knew them but could not remember where from.

Sue said, 'I know you both but don't know from where or your names.'

Arman said, 'Yes Sue, my name is Arman, and this is Sister Rachel, whom you had a lot to do with at the Monastery.'

Sue says, 'Monastery yes, I remember. I was a nun there. Yes, I am a nun, aren't I. I took over from Sister Mary after she died.'

Sister Rachel said, 'No Sue, you are not a nun. The place was under your management, and you handled the bills. You are a film star and was shooting a film when you took ill. Because of a mistaken identity, you believed one of the other film star's daughters was Sarah and couldn't fathom why they took her away from you. You ended up with a nervous breakdown and was hospitalised.

Sue says, 'What is going to happen to me? Where will I stay?'

Arman said, 'You can come back with us to the Monastery and rest up there. We have a medical unit attached to our orphanage, and you can be placed under the care of one of the doctors there. If your doctor at the hospital will release you.'

The nurse says, 'The doctor wants her to stay a week or so to observe how she responds to the treatment and her new medication.'

Arman said, 'That will be fine. You can ring us at the Monastery when you are ready to release her, and one of us will come and pick her up. We will bring clothes for her to change into.' With that, Arman and Sister Rachell gave Sue a kiss and left to go back to their hotel to finish packing and to catch a flight back home.

Sue sat in the hospital, not recalling much. The doctors were concerned that her memory was not coming back to her. She still could not concentrate or recall her past. What she recalled, she forgot quickly. Her retention was very poor.

While Sue was in hospital, she had a visit from her manager, who came to check on her. He hoped she would recover and get back to making movies, but he was taken aback when he found out that she didn't recognise him or remember the film she was working on. He put it down to the type of care she was getting and immediately wanted to transfer her to a clinic that specialised in these cases.

To find a clinic that would take her, he made several phone calls and once one agreed to accept her, he arranged for her transportation there.

Sue was assessed by her new doctors at the clinic as soon as she moved into her private room. They noticed she had received excessive shock treatments and was experiencing distress. They prescribed rest and medication, allowing her time to come to terms with her mental state.

Sue stayed in the hospital for three months. Her memory slowly came back to her. Initially, Sarah and Timothy were remembered by her, and she wondered what had happened to them. She then remembered Sister Rachel and Arman a bit later. She improved over the next two months and was released from hospital and went to her unit to get her thoughts together. Her manager, who had visited weekly, wanted her to go back and finish her movie, but she was not all that infused to go back to work so soon.

He pointed out that her part was the only thing left to film and then it could be shown on the big screen. The film producers were able to lessen her load by bringing in artists that looked like her to do most of the action scenes. All she would have to do was concentrate on the face and speech sections. After weeks of persuasion, she agreed and was flown to the set.

Sue could not produce the sparkle she was previously known for, nor did she look genuinely at playing the part. It got to where the director would have to go over the scene four times before Sue knew what she had to do. She did her part as best as she could with everyone being careful not to put her under pressure, as they all knew she was not ready to take up acting. When it was finally over, the crew broke up and the film sent off for editing and production.

Sue went back to her unit and stayed there for two months, wondering what she could do next. She had not received a phone call or a visit from her agent, so she rang him to see what he had lined up as the next movie. He told Sue that he couldn't help her because her last move didn't make enough money, and many directors knew about her nervous breakdown and didn't want to take a chance with her. He ended the call wishing her success in the future, whatever that may be, and hung up. Sue realised her days as a film star were over and she would have to look elsewhere for a job. But what would she do as acting was the only thing she knew?

She sat in her unit and thought about visiting the Monastery. Despite her inability to recall all the details, she cherished the memories of being there. She decided to give it a go. She packed a bag, booked a flight to the Monastery and headed off to the airport.

CHAPTER 27

Arman was travelling to the west to spread his message when he encountered armed men. They tried to rob him and his companions, wanting to know their identities to demand a ransom.

Arman pulled out his gun and started shooting at the men as soon as they indicated their intensions. The fighting was fierce and four of the bandits were initially killed.

The bandits retreated to an area some distance from Arman. They had weapons, including a rocket launcher, but they didn't know how to use it correctly. Often, they ended up killing their own men instead of Arman's men as the rockets were fired into the air and landed back where the bandits were located.

Arman knew he had to get out of the hole he was in, as they would eventually get their shooting right and launch a rocket at his men. He devised a plan which entailed some of his men circulating left and right of his attackers to get behind them. They would then launch their attack from three sides. If they killed enough of the men, the rest would surrender. The plan was put in action and an equal number of men moved left while another group moved right. Arman and his group started shooting rifles to distract the enemy and ensure they didn't notice what was happening.

Once everyone was in position, they all began shooting and launched their rockets at the opposing force, killing many of them. After about fifteen minutes, the white flag went up and Arman's men stopped shooting. The opposing force stood up and walked out with their hands above their heads.

They were taken to a nearby barn and locked up there until it could be decided what to do with them. Arman questioned the leader and found out they came from a village close to where they were attacked. He decided to go and see what the village looked like and took two of his most able men with him.

They drove into town and walked up the street to see what was there. Surprisingly, there were a lot of shops in the town and a reasonable number of people going about their business. At the end of the street was a christian church, which was boarded up. There was a sign declaring the church was no longer in use by order of the ruling king.

Arman went back to his car and drove to the church. He took some tools out of the back and with the aid of some of his men, took the boards off the windows and doors. As he was doing this, two women came up to him and asked what he was doing. Arman told them and then went back to work. They asked him to stop as the king would send in his troops to regain control and board up the church again. Arman asked why was the king so objectionable towards the christian faith? The women said nothing but turned and walked down the street quickly.

After all the boards were removed, Arman and his men entered the church. Guards were placed at the entry and at the back to ensure no one snuck up on them. When they walked into the church, they noticed its grandeur – stained glass windows with biblical scenes, a gold cross, and crucifixes on the walls. It seemed as if no one had stolen from the church during the period it was boarded up.

As they looked around, a man came in and asked what they were doing in the church. He was from the king, and he had to go back and advise what had happened and what they were doing. Arman advised him they intend to open the church and hold services there. The man said he would advise the king and then left.

Arman continued looking around and was interrupted by two men entering the church and again inquiring as to what was happening. Arman sat in one pew with the men who introduced themselves as the former ministers of the church before it was boarded up. There were four ministers in all and some nuns who assisted in the services and looked after the community until their services were dispensed with by order of the king.

The senior minister was named Brian, and the other minister was Roger. They advised the king had a daughter who was his only child. Her mother died when she was eight and the daughter when she was twelve. The king was a christian but refused to allow the christian religion to be practiced or preached after his daughter died.

He prayed continuously when his wife took ill and was very hurt when his prayers were not answered, and his wife was never cured. He acknowledged God's authority to take her, but after losing his daughter too, he lost hope and rejected Christianity as a scam. To prevent the population from being scammed, he refused to allow them to believe in a God that does not hear prayers or look after his followers. He lost faith in God because he realised the ministers were tricking people into believing in something that didn't exist. All ministers were forced to find another occupation and were prevented from holding any religious service or to preach.

According to the minister, opening the church would make the king reject religion and order the church to be closed or destroyed.

As they were speaking, a truck pulled up outside the church and soldiers piled out of it and stood outside the church. The man in charge could see that armed guards were in position outside the church and no doubt would respond if attacked. He took two guards with him and entered the church, asking who was in charge. Arman was the person he was directed to see, but he had to leave his weapons outside. He handed his rifle and gun to one of his men that accompanied him and entered the church, leaving his two men at the entrance, and walked up to the men sitting in the pew.

Arman introduced himself and said, 'What can I do for you'?

The soldier introduced himself as Mahammad and informed Arman that he was sent by the king. The king wants to know why you removed the timber from the church's windows and doors.

Arman said, 'Will your king agree to my safe return or am I to be arrested and thrown into prison'?

Soldier says, 'My king guarantees your safe return to the church.'

With that, Arman went with the soldier to see the king. The trip took about two hours, as the palace was some distance inland. They drove past many fields with crops ready to be harvested and a few villages with many houses and shopping centres. The area was very prosperous and most of the population seemed well off.

They eventually arrived at the king's palace, which comprised a large building with a racecourse attached. Arman estimated there would be twenty rooms in the palace for guests. He was taken into a large room and asked to be seated. Shortly after, a man walked in and introduced himself as Arthur and put his hand out. Arman stood up and introduced himself, and both men sat down.

Arthur says, 'I understand you have taken off all the timbers boarding up one of the churches. I have given orders that all the Christian churches are to stay closed and would ask you to replace the timber and once you have done this, leave our region.'

Arman said, 'I have come here to spread the word of Jesus Christ not to bow down to suppression or Satin.'

The King says, 'There is no Jesus Christ and the word you mention is made up by ministers who want to profit from religion.'

Arman said, 'Not true, as most ministers do not make a fortune in preaching the bible. Men may hear the word of God and nothing you will do will stop it.'

King says, 'I will instruct my men to take you back to the church and to board up all the windows and doors. You are not welcomed in this area and you should go back to your own region and not interfere in ours.'

Arman said, 'The Lord has directed me to open the church starting with one and then progressively all are to be opened. The people should not fear the word of God but obey it.'

King says, 'They obey my word and not a fictitious god that does not exist. I will not debate your beliefs and my orders. My men will carry out my orders and if there is any opposition, then they have their orders to eliminate this. Do I make myself clear?'

Arman said, 'Yes, we came across one of your units who tried to kill us. Unfortunately for them, we were able to handle the situation and killed some and are holding the others as captives.'

King says, 'Let my soldiers go or I will immediately order troops to where you are holding my men and set them free after they kill you and every one of your men. Do I make myself clear?'

Arman said, 'Yes, very clear. You seem to have gone against Jesus and have found another to follow, namely satin. He is taking over your heart and mind and telling you what to do. My

Lord will not allow this to happen. You must lift your ban on religion and allow the people to worship Jesus Christ our Lord.'

King says, 'And if I do not, your God cannot do anything about it. He could not save my wife and daughter. All He could do was to allow them to die, leaving me with nothing.'

Arman said, 'That is exactly right. You were left with nothing, as you were not a Christian. You idealised your wife's and daughter's beauty and they were christians. The Lord took them back home as their time had come. He wanted to show you that you did not believe in Him and would never join them in heaven and have eternal life. He gave you a wake-up call to change and believe and have the greatest treasure ever able to be received and that is eternal life. All the wealth you have as a king is nothing as compared to eternal life. You can be the richest man in the street and still not match a true Christian's wealth who believes in Jesus Christ and who is guaranteed eternal life. The rich man has it all while he is on this earth and alive and then a thousand years of hell. The poor man struggles on this earth but has internal life in heaven with Jesus Christ. You think about it, as your life depends upon it.'

King said, 'I will not allow you to reopen the christian churches. They are to stay closed, and you are to be arrested and will stay in jail for opening the church without my authority. Arrest him and throw him in jail for two weeks.

Arman said, 'I urge you to reconsider, as the Lord's patience is at an end.'

King says, 'Your god will do nothing. Arrest him.'

Arman said, 'Then let the curse be on you. You will feel pain throughout your body, which will increase each day I am in jail. You will not be able to speak another word and will find it difficult to communicate. This is as the Lord has directed.'

Arman was escorted to jail and locked up in a cell. The king left his chamber and went to lie down for a rest, as he was tired.

When the king rose, he tried to call out to his servant but could not speak. As he got up, he felt his body ache with pain and tried to cry out but could not make a sound. He laid there not able to move, as every time he moved a muscle, it caused extreme pain.

His staff all thought he was having an extended period of rest and left him until they were called. Night fell, and the king laid there, with no one daring to enter because of their previous encounters with his anger. The king laid there all night until the next morning when a servant walked in to see why he had not got up.

With the curtains all closed, preventing any sunlight from entering and lighting up the room; the room was enveloped in darkness. The servant pulled back one flap of the curtain just to see if the king was still asleep. He saw the king staring at him but not moving. He immediately closed the curtain, thinking the king wanted to stay in bed.

After another hour, the staff decided that something was wrong, and two of them went into the room to see what was wrong with the king. They pulled one set of curtains back to let in the sunlight. The king did not move, nor could he say anything. They tried to sit him up, but he was in agony and pushed them away. The servants left, not knowing what to do.

The servants told the captain of the guards what had happened. He accompanied them back to the king's bedroom, and all entered. The captain stood by the king's bedside, waiting for him to speak, but he couldn't say anything or move at all.

The captain did not know what to do, but he was present when Arman put the curse on the King. He went to the jail and confronted Arman.

Captain says, 'Our king is paralysed and cannot move, nor can he speak. You must lift the curse.'

Arman said, 'The curse is not my doing but gods. He is the only one that can lift it.'

Captain says, 'Take him to the king.'

Arman was taken from the jail and with six guards was marched to the where the king laid. He could see the king was in extreme pain and unable to move or say anything. Arman says to the king, 'Speak so your servants know your condition.'

King says, 'I am in extreme pain and could say nothing. Not even order my servant to help.'

Arman said, 'Your voice will stop as soon as I leave you. The Lord has given you time to ask for forgiveness and to confirm you understand he is not just a thought in men's minds.'

King says, 'Yes, yes, I understand. Lift the curse and allow me to continue governing my region.'

Arman said, 'It appears you have still not learnt that the Lord is in charge and not you. Your heart is not towards God, but as soon as you get back on your feet you will destroy all the christian churches. The Lord will not allow this to happen. All the churches are to be reopened, and the people allowed to attend their nominated church. If you do otherwise, you will die.'

King says, 'What, you will come and kill me?'

Arman said, 'Do not mock the Lord. The Lord will lift the curse from you, but should you not obey him, he will take your life. I will leave you, but you have been warned.'

Arman was released from jail and driven back to the church. He and his men then drove home. Arman did not trust the king and wondered what he would do next.

One week later, the king ordered the soldiers to seal up all the churches and burn them, beginning with the one Arman secured.

The captain prepared to burn the church by spreading petrol inside and setting it a light. The king came to watch to make sure his orders were followed. He went inside and could smell the petrol which had been spread inside to accelerate the burn. The captain left the king inside to check on his men, who were ready to light the church up with fire sticks thrown from the front and back doors.

As the captain left the building and crossed the road to give orders to his men, a lightning bolt hit the church, setting it alight. The building exploded into a fireball. As heat buildup, it forced the front and back doors to slam shut, locking the king inside. The building immediately burnt furiously until all that was left was black soot on the ground and bricks that had fallen as the fire took hold. The king died in the fire he ordered. No one could do anything as the building burnt furiously, aided by the accelerants.

A few months after the fire, a new administrator was appointed. They allowed all the churches to open and the people to choose which church they wanted to attend.

Chapter 28

Sue arrived at the Monastery and stood at the front, wondering whether she would be welcomed. She stood there for a minute staring at the building, trying to remember where the various rooms were. She decided not to go in. To her, it was clear that those working there were busy and most likely had already forgotten her. She turned to go back to her car and just as she opened the door to get in, she heard her name being yelled out. She turned to see Sister Rachel running up to her.

Rachel grabbed Sue and gave her a big hug and kiss. Sue stared at her and remembered what she looked like. She says, 'Ra...chel how are you?'

Rachel could see that Sue was not all there, but still hugged her and said, 'What are you doing here? We thought you had gone back to your film career and left us. We enquired at the hospital and were told that your agent had put you in a private hospital, but no one wouldn't tell us where. Come on in and say hallo to your friends.'

Sue got scared and said, 'I better not, as I am sure not too many remember me and besides, they are all busy.'

Rachel says, 'Nonsense. They all will be happy to see you and that you have paid us a visit. Are you staying for a while?'

Sue says, 'Yes, if I may.'

Rachel says, 'Leave your car here and come on in and meet everyone.'

Sue says, 'I am taking you away from your work. I will walk in and catch up with you later.'

Rachel says, 'Yes, I was trying to finish some work for the orphanage when I saw you out the front. I'll just go back in and get it signed off and be back in a minute.'

Rachel left Sue out the front and went in to finish her work, assuming Sue would make her way in as she thought Sue remembered where everyone was located.

Sue stood out the front as Rachel went in to complete her work. She stood there, not knowing where to go. Her mind was blank. She tried to remember, but no matter how much she tried, she couldn't. She stood there thinking, what will they think of me not remembering them? Her nerves finally got the better of her and she got in the car and drove off to her hotel room to ensure she was not embarrassed.

Rachel finished her work and went to see where Sue was. She went in all the areas, including in the orphanage, but could not find her. Finally, she went into the church and noticed

Arman was siting talking to a lady about a christening. She walked up to him and apologises for interrupted and says, 'Have you seen Sue anywhere?'

Arman said, 'Sue, are you joking?'

Rachel says, 'No, I left her at the front of the building and came in to finish some work, thinking she would come in and meet everyone again.'

Arman said, 'Wait until I finish with Mrs Weiss. I cannot understand what is happening.'

Arman took Mrs. Weiss to a small office and scheduled her daughter's christening. He also gave her a leaflet with details about the ceremony. He then walked out with her and made his way to Rachel's office.

Arman said, ' Now what were you saying about Sue?'

Rachel says, 'I saw Sue out the front of the Monastery and went out to greet her. I left her there thinking she would come in and say hallo to all her friends while I finished some work, after which I went back to see where she was. I looked everywhere and couldn't see her, so I went to the church thinking she was with you. But it seems she turned around and went back to where she came from.'

Arman said, 'Last time, she couldn't remember who we were. Most probably she still has a memory problem and by leaving her on her own she could have taken flight as she didn't know where to go.'

Rachel says, 'I never thought about her not remembering us. I should have stayed with her and helped her to remember.'

Arman said, 'It's too late now. We can either ignore her or see if we can find out where she is staying.'

Rachel says, 'I would prefer to find out where she is and get her to come back and see us and tell us what has happened since we last saw her.'

Arman said, 'Well, get on the phone and call all the hotels and find where she is staying. Get some of the other sisters to help you.'

Arman left Rachel and went back to work.

Rachel quickly got four other sisters to help, and each then phoned the hotels in the area to see where Sue was staying. After about fifteen minutes, they located which hotel she was in, and Rachel then ran off to see Arman to tell him.

Arman said, 'Well, what do you want to do?'

Rachel says, 'See if she wants to come back to the Monastery.'

Arman said, 'Then go with one of the other sisters and speak to her.'

Rachel and another sister took one of the staff cars and drove off to where the hotel was located. She knew the room number, so they both took the lift to the floor and walked to the room and knocked.

Sue opened the door and said, 'Can I help you?'

Rachel says, Sue, it's me Rachel. What happened? I thought you were going to see your friends at the Monastery, but it appears you decided not to stay and left.'

Sue says, 'I didn't know where to go and thought I might meet people I don't remember and be embarrassed, as I don't know their names or who they are. I still have difficulty remembering the past. So, when you left me, I decided it was too much for me to do it on my own, so I left.'

Rachel says, 'Well, get your things and come with us back to the Monastery and we will be with you when you meet your friends.'

Sue says, 'I would prefer not to and just rest today. I have booked a flight for tomorrow to go back home, so I will not have the time to see anyone. Thanks for coming.'

With that, Sue stood up and moved to the door and opened it to let Rachel and the other sister out. Rachel got up and walked out of the room to the hallway as the door closed behind her.

Sister says, 'Well, that was a waste of a time.'

Rachel says, 'Yes, but she feels hurt and is running away from us. We must see Arman and get him to talk to Sue. Let's get back.

Rachel droves back to the Monastery and went straight to Arman's office, followed by the other sister. Arman was sitting, attending to some work, and Rachel walked in and told him what had happened.

Arman said, 'Yes, I agree with you. She feels hurt. She thought you were a friend, but you let her down. I am not sure what we can do about it?'

Rachel says, 'You and she always go on well together. She trusts you. If you speak to her, she may change her mind and come back to the Monastery?'

Arman said, 'I don't think so. I think the damage is done and we should give her some time to get over it.'

Rachel burst into tears and was quite upset what Arman had said as she felt she had caused Sue to leave and go back home. She ran out of Arman's office, leaving the other sister there staring at Arman.

Arman said, 'What are you doing here staring at me?'

Sister says, 'Because you let Rachel take the blame for Sue leaving and will not help get her back.'

Arman sat back for a few seconds then said, 'Alright get Rachel. We will all go and speak to Sue.'

Sister went out of the office and found Rachel still crying. She told her that Arman will go to Sue and talk to her, and he wanted both of them to accompany him. With that, Rachel stopped crying and put a smile on her face, and quickly got up and walked to Arman's office, accompanied by the sister. They all went down to the car and Rachel drove off to Sue's hotel.

Upon finding a park just outside the hotel, they entered and made their way towards the lift. They got to Sue's floor and rang the doorbell and waited. After about a minute, the door was opened, and a man appeared at the door in his pyjamas and said, 'What do you want?'

Arman said, 'We understood Sue Pulsar was in this room?'

Man at the door says, 'No Sue Pulsar here. I just arrived and was given this room.' With that, the man closed the door, leaving the three wondering what had happened.

All three caught the lift to the lobby and enquired as to when Sue had booked out.

Receptionist said, 'No our record show. She is still in the hotel on floor thirteen room 13101.

Rachel says, 'Thirteenth floor. We went to twelve no wander she wasn't there. Let's go. Thank you.' And off they all went again, up the lift to the thirteenth floor.

They walked to room 101 and rang the doorbell. After about a minute, Sue appeared at the door, and she recognised Rachel.

Sue says, 'Rachel, I didn't expect you to come back. What can I do for you?'

Rachel says, 'Sue, I feel bad about you not coming and staying at the Monastery. So, we came to see if we could get you to change your mind?'

Arman then stepped forward and says to Sue, 'Do you remember me? I'm Arman.'

Sue said, yes you I remember.' She gave Arman a kiss and singled everyone to come on in.

Everyone went in and sat down either on the bed or a chair.

Arman said, 'Sue, we would like you to come back with us to the Monastery and tell everyone what had happened as they are all your friends and care about you. They all want to know what has happened to you.'

Sue hesitated and then said, 'Unfortunately, I still suffer memory loss and sometimes forget what I am saying or thinking. It is a byproduct of the shock therapy. I stood at the Monastery and couldn't remember where I was and where things were located. I panicked and left, deciding to go back home. My flight is scheduled for tomorrow morning.

Arman said, 'Can't you put it off? We all would like to see you and hear what had happened. Spend time with you and get your help in fixing up the books.'

Sue says, 'I don't think I can be much help there, but would like to go back to see if my memory comes back.'

Arman said, 'Good. Now that we have you back, just pack up your things and let's get out of the hotel and back to our own community. Girls, help Sue pack her bags.'

Sue says, 'No need. I have already packed my things for an early flight home tomorrow.'

Arman said, 'Just phone up and cancel your flight and we will be on our way.'

Sue cancelled her flight, checked out of the hotel, and left for the Monastery with everyone helping carry her bags.

CHAPTER 29

Sue stood outside the Monastery, staring out with her eyes fixed on its large entrance. Arman saw she was scarred and took her by the hand. He walked in with her and stood at the entrance to let her get her bearings.

She stood for a moment, then Sue walked in, still holding Arman's hand, not willing to venture in by herself. Arman took her to all the various halls and rooms. Some Sue remembered, while other parts seemed new to her. She remembered the orphanage but not the medical centre or hospital. She met many people who mostly knew her, but she had no memory of them. They had heard of her illness and understood.

Finally, Arman took Sue to the church and sat her down in a pew. Sue remembered the cross and what had happened to Arman. She sat there for a minute and the donkey came in and stood in front of the cross and bowed. Sue remembered the donkey and the times she used to pat it and groom him.

Sue sat there for a moment, then the donkey turned and walked up to Sue, giving her a nudge and then a big kiss on her check. She was thrilled that he remembered her and got up and gave the donkey a big hug.

The donkey sensed Sue was not right and as she hugged him, he tried to take her to the cross, but she let go of him. The donkey walked out, leaving Sue. She sat down, staring at the cross, remembering what it had done for Arman and others. She sat there and then stood up and walked out with Arman in hand.

Sue decided to go to her room and rest, as she had a big day roaming around and meeting everyone again. Arman left her and went to finish some work. He sat in his office for two hours, then thought it best to check on Sue, so he went up to her room and listened to see if he could hear her moving around. Nothing, so he knocked, and Sue opened the door.

Armen says, 'How do you feel? If you're alright, you can give me a hand at tonight's service as you use too'.

Sue said, 'I don't remember what must be done. You will have to ask one of the sisters.

Arman said, 'No, they are always busy with the children at the orphanage in the evenings, either washing the children or feeding them, so they do not have the time. Just sit and watch and I am sure it will come back to you.'

Both Sue and Arman went into the kitchen to have their meals. Sue ate most of her dinner but could not finish it all. Afterwards, she went back to her room to freshen up and so did Arman, who also put on his priestly robes.

Arman then went to Sue's room, and both went down to the church. Sue sat in the front pew looking at the service progressing and slowly began to remember what she used to do in the past. She watched Arman and remembered the prays he read, knowing she had heard them before. She sat there mainly looking at the cross and the number of people that came before it to pray and bow, showing their reverence.

The service ended within the hour, and Arman took Sue out to show her what was happening in both the orphanage and the expansion of the hospital. They walked through the orphanage, stopping as sisters greeted Sue, who did not remember most of them. Most would say their names and Sue would acknowledge whether she remembered them. Mostly she didn't.

Arman took Sue through the hospital and clinic and Sue was surprised at the size of the hospital and the number of wards, and all were full. There were doctors and nurses around, even at this late hour. After a while, Arman sensed Sue was tired and took her back to her room. She did not remember where it was and would have got lost if left to her own resources. Arman left Sue to either watch television or go to bed. Sue chose to have an early night as she was worn out. Arman went to finish some work.

The next morning, Rachel came to Sue's room and together they went down for breakfast. Afterwards, Sue stayed with Rachel or one of the other sisters.

That evening, Arman took Sue to where Sarah and Timothy were laid to rest. She immediately became emotional and had to be carried from there. A doctor was called, who gave her a sedative to calm her down. It lasted through the night and allowed her to regain her composure for the next morning.

Over several weeks, Sue familiarised herself with the buildings and layout of the complex.

Slowly, things came back to her. One thing she seemed not to have forgotten was the grave of Sarah and Timothy. When she first went to visit them, she would burst into tears and fell on her knees, sobbing over their graves. She managed to get to her feet and control her emotions. She never forgot them even in the worst of her mental episodes.

Sue would visit the grave of Sarah and Timothy every couple of days and put fresh flowers on them. She felt guilty for not adopting the children earlier and blamed herself for their tragic fate.

Sue enjoyed the freedom of the Monastery and the diversity of activity she could get involved in. She mostly enjoyed looking after the orphanage and helping with the children. It helped get her mind off what happed to Sarah and Timothy and her own limitations and memory problems.

CHAPTER 30

Sue was not feeling the best and decided to see a doctor at the clinic. She made an appointment and went to see him at the designated time. He examined her thoroughly and considered her medical history. He strongly disagreed with the doctors' choice to give her shock treatment.

The doctor could find nothing physically wrong with Sue and sent her off for blood tests and X-Rays. All came back negative. They decided to wait and see if anything showed up over time. She was close by so they could observe her. They did say that in their opinion, they thought it was a mental condition rather than a physical one.

Over time, Sue became moodier and would be seen staring at nothing, as if she had depression. Doctors gave her medication for depression, but it did not seem to help. Arman also noticed a change in Sue and wondered what the problem was. He would try to accompany her wherever she went to help her, but she became objectionable and would get into a war of words before storming off. Her mood had changed and no doubt so had her mind.

Sue knew something was not right, but she did not know what was affecting her. She also noticed she was reverting to her previous position in not believing in God, as she had been when a film star. She pondered if an evil spirit had entered her, as she tried to push Jesus Christ out of her mind. However, it was his name and image that gave her solace during her stay in the mental hospital and during shock treatment. He stayed with her then, and she was not willing to give him up now, even though she still declared herself an atheist. She continually had reflections of Sister Mary telling her to be careful the devil has got her, whatever that meant. It was all too confusing for Sue.

Sue went through her daily routine and finally to bed and rest. One night, she saw Sister Mary and the devil arguing over Sue's soul. The devil grabbed a cross from the church and used it to kill Sister Mary. Sue would immediately wake up in a sweat and found it hard to go back to sleep. She decided to talk to Arman about it and the next morning went to his office to discuss her dream.

Arman believed that the recurring dream could be Sister Mary's way of warning Sue about the devil's interest in her. When you were a film star, you frequently expressed disbelief in Jesus Christ. Sister Mary attempted to convince you about his existence and the benefits of embracing christianity. When you got sick, you turned to Christ for strength to overcome your mental illness and shock treatment, even though you hadn't thought of it before. You told me about this when you came back to the Monastery. What Mary is telling you is the devil is making a play to keep you away from Christ and he will not stop at anything, even killing, to get you out of here and back to your previous self.'

Sue left Arman and went to the church to think about what Arman had said. There she could sit and think, with no one interrupting her.

She sat there and wondered how the devil managed to rip the cross off its base and hit and kill Sister Mary. No one was around, so she went up to the cross and knelt to look at the base. She thought to herself 'It would be impossible to remove it from its base'. As she was getting up, she slipped and put both of her arms on the cross. Immediately, she felt a spirit going through her as a bolt of lightning had gone through her. She stood there while her body was shaking, yet her mind was clear, and she saw Jesus with Mary standing alongside him. She tried to speak but could not.

As Sue was hanging onto the cross, Arman came into church and could see her leaning over the cross, shaking. He moved towards Sue but could not get near her. There was a barrier between them. He could only look on as she continually moved her mouth as if she was speaking to someone. Then she fell to the floor momentarily, not moving. Arman rushed over to her and picked her up and sat her in a pew.

Arman said, 'Sue, are you alright? Can you hear me?'

Sue replies, 'Yes Arman, I am alright. I just been speaking to Sister Mary and Jesus.'

Arman said, 'You better tell me what has happened. But first I will get you to the clinic, so they can check you over.'

Sue says, 'No, that won't be needed. What have you lost your faith?'

Arman said, 'What happened when you were anchored to the cross?'.

Sue said, 'I was before God and at his right were Jesus Christ and Sister Mary. She told me she still wants me to take over from her and I should be careful, as the devil is after my soul. Then God says, 'I will teach you about the bible's history' and showed what happened from creation to Jesus' resurrection. I was then advised not to worry about the loss of memory or the shock treatment, as I have been made anew. I then could let go and fell at the base of the cross.'

Arman said, 'It sounds like you had a similar trip like I had. What are you going to do?'.

Sue says, 'It seems my memory has been restored and I can function as I had before the shock therapy. I want to get hold of that manager of mine and see if we can reshoot the last part of my film that went terribly wrong and which made me look terrible. That should take two weeks and then come back and take it from there'.

Arman said, 'Was anything told to you?'

Sue says, 'Yes, Mary said be careful as the devil was knocking at my door and would do anything to prevent me from becoming a christian.'

Jesus says, 'You are to go out and be my voice.'

Arman said, 'So what are you going to do?'

Sue says, 'Become a christian when I return from finishing the film. When I return you will baptise me as I haven't been baptised yet'.

Arman said, 'Didn't your parents baptise you when you were a child?'.

Sue says, 'No, neither of my parents were religious nor did they take the time to go to church and find out what it means to be a christian'?

Arman said, 'So you will go away again, I see'?

Sue says, 'only for two weeks to finish the last part of my film. I owe it to the producers.'

Arman said, 'I will baptise you now.'

With that, Arman took Sue up to the main section of the church and into a private office. He prepared the vases with water and oil and finally said a pray and baptised Sue in the name of the Father.

Sue left Arman and made a phone call to her manager, who was surprised to hear from her and who was very happy to see she had recovered. Sue did not tell him what had happened, but asked whether she could redo the last few scenes of her last move to ensure the move was commercially viable. The manager made some phone calls, and the producers and directors were excited to collaborate because the previous filming was so bad that they couldn't sell the film.

Sue made her arrangements to fly off and agreed to return to the Monastery within a fortnight.

Everyone heard what had happened to Sue and the Cross and that she regained her health and was back to her normal self.

CHAPTER 31

The director yells out 'action' and Sue and the other actors went through their motions until the word "cut' was yelled out by the director. This went on for a week and a half until the director was happy with all the scenes. The film would then be cut with the last pieces added to the full-length film. Sue was happy with what she had done, and this would reflect favourably on her career. Rather than wait around, she flew to her unit and decided to rest for a few days. On the second day, she received a call from a TV show asking if they could interview her about her film. She agreed, and a crew was despatched to her unit for the interview. It went well and everyone was happy to see her back on the screen, performing with her great smile, poise, and dedication.

Sue took a walk to clear her head. She went down the street and passed a church which had people entering. Curious about what was happening, she made the choice to go in and see. She discovered a seat close to the front and patiently waited. After approximately five minutes, a minister emerged, and the service begun.

Sue noticed that the minister was not interpreting the bible correctly and was misleading the congregation. He continued for about ten minutes, then Sue objected to his sermon. She stood up and said, 'Excuse me, why are you misinterpreting the bible or are you rewriting the bible?'

The Minister says, 'Stop interrupting me and sit down'.

Sue said, 'I will if you tell us the truth and stop misrepresenting the bible'.

The audience clapped, and Sue stood up and headed for the pulpit. The minister immediately left the pulpit and headed for the exit and safety.

Sue, standing in the pulpit, says, 'This man doesn't know what he is saying or knows and intentionally is misleading the congregation to do the devil's work. He should not be a minister. The passage that he is preaching says......' Sue continues for about an hour and concluded with a prayer. Everyone applauded her. She waited until everyone left and then went out of the church and home.

Shortly afterwards, she received phone calls from radio and TV stations asking how she knew the bible and what had transacted at the church. While explaining, she made it clear that what had happened was unacceptable and that she would not accept a minister misrepresenting the bible. To her credit, she could discuss the bible and debate issues with academics and ministers, which led to her being asked to appear on several shows.

She agreed to appear and conduct a service on a Sunday in a famous church. During her sermon, she talked about a controversial passage in the Bible and shared her interpretation and its impact on people's lives. The service was telecast in several states. Everyone marvelled at the way the film star handled herself and the knowledge she had about the bible and Jesus Christ.

Sue gained confidence in her ability to preach the word to large audiences. Her appearance in films allowed her to be well known and respected and in demand. She gained a reputation as a speaker and found it hard when her period was up, and she had to return to the Monastery to attend to her bookkeeping.

Sue remembered her promise to return within two weeks, so she cut short all the appearances requested of her and booked her flight back to the Monastery. There will be other times when she could spend more time preaching the word.

The next day she was back at her desk in the Monastery attending to her work. Arman was going north again to preach the word, and she decided to go with him to assist. He agreed to her accompanying him, against his better judgement, as the tribes were still waging war against each other to gain more territory.

A week later, they headed off northwest to spread the word. They drove through very lush lands, which showed the people had faith in the Lord and he looked upon them with love and grace.

After six hours of travelling, the landscape changed to a dried and harsh arid land that hadn't seen rain for many years. As they continued their journey, it became apparent that the drought had taken hold, and the people would experience hunger and thirst caused by the drought. No animals were visible, not even a bird. They finally reached their destination, which was a township called Grace. They drove through the township. Not a person was visible. No dogs were roaming the streets, nor were there any birds flying around.

A large church, which was prosperous and well-supported in its day, stood at the end of the town. The minister asked Arman to drop in if he was in the area, never expecting he would take up the invitation. They parked their cars around the back and Arman and his men got out of the cars and approached the church. The front door wasn't locked, so they walked in and looked around. They checked the rear rooms, and no one could be found.

Six months ago, the local minister contacted Arman by email to talk about self-determination and moral choices without God. Two years ago, the people agreed to adopt same sex marriages, abortion and euthanasia amongst several other contentious matters. The State had legislated to enable these things to happen even though they were forbidden in the bible.

The people allowed the State to decide what they should do in these matters and did not see why they needed a church or follow Christ. Most were well off and considered they had gained their affluence through their own efforts and by making the right decision, not by the grace of God. The local two ministers were shot dead in a scuffle some five months ago and only three people turned up at their funerals.

Arman went back into the church and sat in a pew, considering what he should do. As he sat there, several people came into the church asking what they were doing there. These people lived closed by and wanted the church to reopen, but the majority didn't want this to happen. They advised the last two ministers were shot while they were holding a service and were buried in a pauper's grave.

Arman decided since they came all this way that they should at least hold a service for those who wanted to worship Christ. He put a notice out the front of the church on the notice board, advising the day and time of the next service. He walked around so he could see the extent of the drought, which was severe.

They made themselves comfortable in the back rooms and cooked themselves a meal and went to bed early so they could get an early start the next morning. Guards were left to secure the premises and to ensure no one surprised them during the night.

The next morning, they all had breakfast, showered and headed off to inspect the countryside. Some men were left behind to ensure no one bunt the church down.

As they drove along the dirt road, they could see the land was dry and barren and began opening as the drought took hold. They passed several farms and decided to call into the next one to see what the occupants had to say. When they arrived at the farmhouse, they noticed an absence of people. They walked up to the barn and opened it and walked around. There were several bales of hay, but no animals or people around.

They went up to the farmhouse and pressed the doorbell. There was no answer, so they tried the door and found it was unlocked. They walked in and could see that no one had lived in the house for some time. While looking around the paddocks, they discovered a mound of animal bones, showing that the animals had been gathered, shot, and left to decay. Not a soul could be seen. They went back and stay in the barn for the night before heading back into town. As they drove in near the church, they noticed people out the front of the church reading the sign. When they approached them, they asked what had happened to the previous minister. They were told and warned that most people were against the church opening and did not want the return of religion. They did not believe in God and the drought was a clear sign in their minds that there was no God.

Armen asked what the minority wanted and was told they wanted a church with a minister who believed in Christ and who didn't want to change the bible.

He told them he was holding a service that evening, and they were welcomed to attend. He instructed them to inform all their neighbours to come to the service, and not fear God.

Sue and the other men accompanied him as they entered the church to prepare and sweep it. Electricity was still available in the church, enabling it to be cleaned and the pews dusted down. By the evening, it looked as though it was a place of worship and not a large barn, even though it might have some two-legged sheep in it during the service.

People moved into the church at around five o'clock. Within half an hour, the church was full, and people had to stand at the back or outside of the church.

Arman came out to begin the service assisted by Sue. His men were strategically positioned both inside and outside the church to prevent any disturbances. They were given strict orders to use force if necessary. The service began and about halfway through the service, some men who were seated in the front pews stood up and yelled out to stop the service. They immediately pulled out their guns and aimed them at Arman and Sue.

Arman's men, sensing this was going to be trouble, drew their guns and fired at the men, killing them instantly. Some in the crowd screamed while others were trying to get away. A man stood up in the pew and said, 'Why should we pray to God when he doesn't care about us? Look at the extent of the drought. Nothing is alive, not a blade of grass. We are being punished for no reason'.

Arman stepped forward and said, 'You lie to me as you have lied to the Lord and to yourselves.' Knowing that what they say was completely wrong; 'You allowed your ministers to make their own interpretation of the bible and took no action to prevent them from doing so. Despite contradicting biblical teachings, you supported the State's decision to legalize same-sex marriages, abortion, euthanasia, and more. You were the masters and accordingly told God to get out of your lives. None of you defended the faith. You said you did not want Christ in your lives, you were doing so well on your own, so He heard you and left you to your own devices. You became masters of your own destiny.

Since you were in control of your lives, you should have made the weather rain on your patch of earth. None of you could, yet you were all quick to declare to the Lord that you were in control and you didn't need Jesus. Well, why are you crying out now? You got what you asked for. The Lord will not show his face to you until you fall on your knees and repent, asking for his forgiveness.

One patron sitting in the pew yells out, 'Well, He will wait a long time.'

Arman said, 'You still think you have the upper hand? Then let me say the drought will intensify and water will dry up within the next two weeks. Those who can buy in water will survive for a short period. Those who have no money will die and will come face to face with Jesus. Since you said you did not want to know him, he will honour your wishes and send you to hell for a thousand years.'

Everyone sat down and no further comments were made. The service finished and all the patrons moved out of the church and made their way home. None stayed back to thank Arman for the service nor to ask the Lord for forgiveness. There was no doubt that pride ruled their lives.

Arman's men took the dead bodies out to the cemetery for burial. They locked up the church, and all stayed there that night fearing retribution from those who did not want a church in town.

The next morning, everyone rose early and packed up their things, had breakfast and took off for home. Unbearable heat in the vehicles made the trip exhausting. The guards who were on duty during the night tried to get some sleep, but it was too hot with no breeze to cool them down.

Eventually, they got out of the drought area and were glad to be in a more comfortable environment. A few hours later, they arrived at the Monastery, and everyone went to their rooms to unpack and rest.

A few weeks had passed and one tribesman who had gone to the northern area to trade, upon returning, advised Arman that some patrons had burnt the church down.

Arman knew their actions would bring trouble to the community as everyone stood back and allowed it to happen. Since they did not believe in Christ, they would all pay the price. Inactivity and reliance on others to do the right thing always leads to all suffering the same faith.

CHAPTER 32

Sue hurried as she had to catch a flight to America to fulfill several lecture engagements, which she committed herself to. Her responsibility included speaking at several services on various topics of interest. She had gained a reputation as a speaker and could debate any part of the bible with academics and theologians. Many theologians were puzzled by her knowledge of Christ and the Bible, considering she was a film star with no biblical film roles or formal religious education.

Sue dedicated her time to speaking about the bible at rallies and christian services and helping churches and schools who did not have a minister. On this occasion, Sue would be away for a week and had four engagements to fulfill in the States.

She started off in Boston, where there was a rally of three thousand people to encourage more young people to be involved in the church. Her speech was on the subject 'Defend the word'. As she began, a young man stood up and yells out, 'You're wasting your time. There is no God. Pray as much as you will, it makes no difference'.

Sue asked the man to come up to the stage. She requested he advise everyone what was troubling him to reach such a conclusion. The man advised, his wife had just died of cancer, leaving him with three young children. He used to go to church with his wife every Sunday and she believed in Christ. Because he didn't believe he was a Christian, he advised he went along for the ride. He adored his wife, and she was his strength and joy. From the time he found out his wife had cancer to her death, was four months. He prayed daily that she would be cured. Nothing happened except the chemotherapy did nothing and she died shortly thereafter.

The man was sobbing as he revealed his story, and you could see the anger he had built up against God. His parents that were with him tried to tell him otherwise, but he believed he knew best. He kept shouting out, 'It is a fraud! Don't believe any of them.'

Sue asked whether he had the autopsy report on his wife, which he had in his bag. After ransacking it, he handed over to her. Sue skimmed through it and asked him whether he had read it. Which he replies, 'Why should I? She is dead.'

Sue got permission from the man to disclose the autopsy report details. She then informed the audience that it stated his wife had an advanced and excruciating cancer for which there was no cure. Chemotherapy has no effect on it. 'Your wife died before this aggressive cancer took hold of her body, ensuring she did not suffer a long and agonising period to her death. The autopsy report made it clear she died of a different tumour and not of the aggressive one.'

'We all will die, and everyone here knows this. I can only assume you idealised your wife and she, in fact, took the place of God in your life. You said that you only went to church to keep your wife happy and to give her company. God wants you to believe in Him with all your heart and soul. He took your wife early to prevent you and your family from going through the prolonged and agonising death of your wife. She is in a better place now, hoping you will change and believe in God and bring your children up as christians. Your wife was spared by God from having to go through a torturous death. He wants you to be a christian and eventually when your time comes to be in heaven with your wife and God. The man was sobbing, and his parents came to the stage and helped him back to his pew.

CHAPTER 33

Sue had received several invitations to speak at rallies and at large congregational churches. She was going through her list of those she would consider as worthwhile and those who had more money than cause. While going through her list, Arman entered her office and mentioned that he was going to the children's grave site to place flowers. He asked if Sue would like to join him. She agreed, and both went off to buy some flowers.

Half an hour later, both were at the site. The headstone read 'Here lies Sarah and Timothy. Always in our hearts.'

Sue sobbed as she put her flowers down on Sarah's grave. Arman put his bunch on Timothy's grave. Both bowed their heads and said a prey and stood back thinking if only we acted differently. If only they knew what was happening right under their noses. They stayed awhile and then started to walk back to the car when Arman said, 'What is the list you are working on?'.

Sue said, 'I have received several invitations to speak at various venues and I am forced to cut back on the number I can handle. Those I cannot do; I will write to and advise them accordingly and make firm appointments with the others.

Arman said, 'Maybe I should join you and take those you cannot do and in that way we can both spread the Word.'

Sue says, 'That is a great idea. We can both take a mixture of large and small venues, ensuring everyone hears us.'

Sue wrote to those venues she decided not to speak at and invited them to take Arman, who was also accompanying her. They agreed, and both made plans to go to the States for a quick two-week trip to spread the Word.

With bags packed, the Apostles headed off to the airport, leaving the sisters to run the Monastery for the next two weeks and Nicholas to handle the services.

The plan was to speak at the various functions and then meetup as if they were crossing each other's paths. Sue stayed where she landed, but Arman had to get on a connecting flight to his destination.

Sue stayed at a nearby hotel, freshened up, and then took a taxi to the university. She was scheduled to speak to a crowd of five thousand students about abortion. This topic is very political and emotional, and people have strong opinions based on their personal views about abortion.

She met with the Dean and various Vice Presidents and professors who were also going to speak in support of abortions. They each set out the areas they were supporting and the major theme of their speech. This way no one could be ambushed, and each could take the other person's theme and raise arguments in opposition to it. That way, the presentation would cover both sides of the arguments. The presentation was to be held that evening at eight. After staying for an hour, Sue went back to her hotel room to get a bite to eat and rest up.

Once in her room, she ordered room service and had a light meal brought up. She ate all that was ordered and after the plates were collected, Sue went to bed for a quick nap.

The clock rang on time and Sue got out of bed and showered, dressed, and took care of her hair and makeup. She then caught a cab to the university.

As she approached the main building, she could see there was a large crowd streaming into the build. It looked like a fiery evening.

She went to the convention room where the Dean and the other speakers were assembled, ready to take their positions on stage. She chatted with them, getting a better understanding of the theme they were presenting. After having a cup of coffee, all were asked to come on stage as they were being introduced.

The host came on stage and gave a warm welcome to everyone in attendance, as well as those watching from home, including viewers abroad. One by one, the speakers were named and as they came on stage, they shook the MC's hand and sat in a seat designated to them. Last was Sue, who was described as opposing the trend. She was heckled as she came on stage. The crowd didn't want to hear the opposing view.

Sue stood there for a minute while being introduced, looking at the placards and students standing heckling her.

She sat in her seat and said a short pray asking Jesus to give her wisdom and help her make a good presentation in support of the bible's view.

The first speaker was asked to present his speech, and he stood up and moved to the podium and placed his papers on the lectern. He immediately went on the attack on the Supreme Court's decision in Roe v Wade to the applause of the crowd.

The second speaker then advanced the view of legalising abortions and confirmed it was a woman's right to decide what happens to her body. The audience screamed in support, and it was obvious the speakers who taught at the university were not willing to rock the boat.

Next was Sue's turn. She stood on the podium and placed her notes on the lectern. The crowd roared and the placards went up, stating it was a woman's right to decide what happened to her body.

Sue looked at the crowd momentarily and said, 'You say it is a woman's right as to what she does with her body. I say get your facts right as we are not arguing here as to the woman's rights but the right of a woman to kill an unborn child. It's easier to blend the two topics together, which helps avoid addressing the real issue: does a woman have the right to abort a foetus? This argument is a separate argument as to the right of the foetus. The right of an unborn child.'

Abortions were unthinkable to Israelian women in biblical times. Why? Because children were thought of as God's gift to them. Childness was seen as a curse, as barrenness would mean the extinction of the family name.

Our legal system does not recognise an absolute right over a woman's body.

A woman can prevent pregnancy by abstaining from having sex. It is one hundred percent effective not requiring an abortion.

'Every abortion result in a foetus, an unborn child, being killed. When removed from the womb, the foetus can be seen to have a heartbeat and blood is moving around the body. To have an abortion is to kill the foetus. The only reason you don't get sentenced to life imprisonment for doing this act is the State allows you to get off scot-free, but the bible does not. By having an abortion, you are killing an unborn child.'

'You are going against the teaching of the bible. To safeguard your own sanity and sins, you are saying we do not want to follow the bible but will allow the State to control all aspects of our lives. The bible is giving you the freedom to run your own life but has strict rules regarding abortion. If allowed, the State will control your lives and dictate what you can and cannot do.'

'It is God who gives life, not the women. By having an abortion, you are in fact rejecting the bible's teaching, the word of Jesus Christ and the gift of a life.'

'You are saying I do not want the freedom of choice the bible gives me but have a State that dictates what I can or cannot do with my life through Law.'

'The law should make it mandatory that the person who has an abortion should personally kill their child and not leave it up to a stranger to do this for them. They should witness the heartbeat stopping. If they caused the pregnancy, they should be the ones to end the life of the foetus instead of involving a stranger to do this murderous act.'

'You stand before me waving your stupid placards declaring your rights, but what about the rights of the foetus, your baby? Yes, it is your body, but we are not arguing about your gut but the baby that lives within you. No wonder so many women have mental problems once they abort their pregnancy. They eventually realise they were tricked into thinking it was easy to get away with getting an abortion with no consequences. No one will know.'

'You know, and you show it. Your soul knows it.'

'The bible doesn't allow abortions unless it is necessary to save the life of the mother. If you don't want the baby, there are couples out there who will take the baby off your hands at birth and bring it up as if it was their own. They, for several reasons, cannot have children and look to those who do not want their babies to give them up for adoption.'

The crowd became quitter, and the placards were lowered. One in the crowd yells out, 'That is all wrong, the foetus doesn't have any features at the earl stage.'

Sue said, 'Then you are pregnant and quite willing to kill your baby, are you?'

The heckler says, 'I don't have to. The doctors will do it for me.'

Sue says, 'How many pregnancies have you already aborted?'

Heckler says, 'Three.'

Sue said, 'You are surely not a christian nor a person who cares about life. You go from partner to partner, trying to fill your life with some sort of purpose, and think the only way to gain a partner is to sleep with them. You're a 'Jessabell' and will end up in hell unless you take control of your sinful action. Rather than doing what is right, you follow the commands of the devil.'

The woman sat down and could be seen crying.

Sue said, 'The decision of the Supreme Court to overturn the decision of Roe v Wade was right as the law allowing abortions was wrong. It was a law enabling the killing of the foetus. Some States have enacted their own laws allowing abortion, but this is made to gain votes rather than making the right decision.'

The State is meddling in religion, which teaches moral values. Meanwhile, the State is letting people off the hook for their actions by using ethical reasoning instead of moral reasoning. These people are protected by legislation which most times is contrary to the teaching of the bible. However, it is our inner selves that truly react and can cause our downfall. All the State cares about is your vote, allowing those with wealth to manipulate politicians and control your life.'

Sue then sat down. There was no applause, as with the other two speakers.

The master of ceremonies concluded the session, and everyone moved out of the auditorium.

Sue was appreciated for attending and presenting, but she won't be asked to return to the university because they can't handle the truth. It is the 'WOC' that they desire and educate their students accordingly.

Sue went back to her hotel and to bed. The next morning, she had an early breakfast and flew off to catch up with Arman, who was yet to make his presentation.

CHAPTER 34

Arman was waiting for Sue at the airport, pacing up and down looking at the shop fronts. He noticed several elderly travellers were around and wondered what they thought about the right to end their own lives rather than allow the laws of nature to dictate when they were to die.

Sue finally exited the plane and waved to Arman as she walked down the gangplank. Arman saw her and moved behind the barrier as she came out.

Sue gave Arman a big hug, and both went down to collect Sues bag from the carousel and a cab to the hotel. Once at the hotel, Arman left Sue to freshen up.

Sue unpacked her bag and went to the bathroom to wash her face. Once she had freshened up, she went to Arman's room, which was on the same floor, and knocked on the door. Arman let Sue in, and both went into a small room, which was the study. Arman advised Sue he was to make his presentation the next day and that most people he spoke to were in favour of euthanasia, including ministers of the church. The practice was contrary to the teachings of the bible but most states in

America had legislated to allow it to happen, especially with a terminal illness.

Arman and Sue discussed the points that should be made and then went down to the restaurant to have dinner. Afterwards, they went to their rooms to get a good night's sleep.

The next morning, they both toured the city and, in the afternoon, made their way to the venue for the debate. There were two speakers in this instance. One was a medical professor presenting the argument for acceptance of euthanasia and Arman, who was to present the contrary argument.

The professor was introduced first and made a reasonable case for euthanasia. Arman was then introduced and moved to the podium and placed his notes on the lectern.

Arman said, 'Does euthanasia make up an act of assisted suicide, or an act of murder? Or mercy killing? The Bible specifically condemns murder. Euthanasia involves premeditated intent and therefore, should be seen as a criminal act.'

'The argument as to who presses the button or who takes the tablet is irrelevant. Those people who assist the person to die are intentionally setting up a method to murder the person and, as such, should be prosecuted under the Act for murder.'

'The right to euthanize is to deny God his sovereign right to end a life. He decides when you are born and should decide when your time is up, not you who had no say in your coming.'

'With modern medicine, a person can live reasonably well and out of pain and can take advantage of new discoveries.

Euthanasia prevents the use of any invention or medicine. It is final.'

'To allow euthanasia, you are starting the process where initially you may end your life. It then will develop into the State deciding and then progressing onto setting parameters as to who is to be euthanized. The criterion will be to ensure limited resources are applied to the greater need, but this is only an excuse to remove the disabled, elderly, terminally ill and those that society deems who are not worthy of life.'

'The Bible teaches we are created in the image of God and therefore have dignity and value to society. Human life is sacred and should not be ended merely because life is difficult or inconvenient.'

'Society must not place an arbitrary standard of quality above God's absolute standard of human value and worth. Euthanasia should be rejected. To give the State more control over our lives is to shackle us with more laws and controls, which one day will cause the destruction of a good percentage of the population while progressively devalue life generally.'

'The important question is whether you support the Bible and Jesus Christ's teachings or if you've given up your freedom to follow the State. Giving more power to the State means losing democratic rights.'

As Arman gathered his papers and moved off the podium, a man walked on the stage, pulled a gun out of his pocket, and shot Arman in the chest. Arman collapsed on one knee, then fell face down on the stage. The MC ran up to him and turned him over, but it was obvious Arman was dead shot through the heart. Blood was pouring out of his body.

Sue, who was sitting in the audience, didn't believe what she had just seen and was motionless for a few seconds. She then stood up quickly and ran to the stage. Someone yelled out to call the ambulance and police.

Sue knelt over Arman's motionless body, grabbing and hugging him, crying uncontrollably as she held onto him. She couldn't believe that someone chosen by God could be killed while spreading the word.

Sue had to be sedated, as she was hysterical and wouldn't leave Arman's side. As the drug took effect, she leaned over him and gave Arman one last kiss and collapsed over him.

They took her to the local hospital, who transferred her to the psychiatric ward so the appropriate doctors could treat her. She was sedated for three days and then given two days to rest before being discharged from the hospital. She was advised not to return to work until she had processed Arman's death and accepted the fact he was dead.

Sue called the Monastery to inform them about the situation. She mentioned she was working on getting Arman's body back to the Monastery but could not leave the mental hospital. Arman's men, who did not accompany him to America, were deeply upset and blamed themselves for not being there to protect him.

All at the Monastery heard what had happened, and they arranged a pray session for Arman. An Apostle killed while spreading the word. No one could understand why this happened. No doubt, many looked upon this to be a test of faith.

Two of Arman's men flew over to the States to help Sue, as they knew she would not be in any condition to handle the transfer of his body back to the Monastery by herself. When they spoke to her, she could barely speak without bursting into uncontrollable crying, making it hard to understand what she was trying to say.

The two men who were known to Sue arrived on the day Sue was being discharged from the hospital. They went to the hospital and helped her back to the hotel.

Once in the hotel, Sue burst into tears and could not stop crying, as she could not understand why the Lord allowed Arman an apostle to be gunned down in such a brutal way.

Some days had passed and eventually, the coroner released Arman's body, and it was flown back to the Monastery for burial. All at the monastery stood in line with their heads bowed as his body was taken from the hearse into the church, ready for his funeral.

An argument developed when Arman's parents wanted him to be buried in his hometown, where he grew up and where most of his relatives lived. Sue finally agreed to this, and arrangements were made to transfer the body to his hometown.

Sue decided to travel to the region where Arman came from to attend his funeral and speak to his parents. She wanted to thank them for their support and encourage them to stop guarding the Monastery. She intended to propose the men focus on their families instead of risking their lives as bodyguards.

The killer claimed insanity and two psychiatrists supported his plea, recommending he never be released or paroled. He stayed in a secure psychiatric hospital for two months before being violently killed by another patient whom he picked a fight with.

CHAPTER 35

The escort was hastily assembled and before Sue could say another word; they were off to Arman's village to deliver his body to his parents. The trip took some ten hours to get to the region.

As they drove through the landscape, it was obvious the Lord blessed the region, for it was lush and heavily stocked with sheep and cattle. They arrived at a vibrant city and drove through it, heading towards a grand estate with steel gates some five miles out of town.

When they reached the entrance of the mansion, they advised who they were, and the gats automatically opened. They drove up to the house, noting that there were heavily armed guards with rifles stationed every fifty feet apart along the driveway.

When the car stopped, Sue got out and was escorted to the house and ushered inside. In the foyer was a man and women who seemed to be in their sixties and several other younger persons. They all introduced themselves to Sue and accompanied her into a large room which had chairs and several smaller tables. Sue was asked to sit down and invited to have tea, which she was thankful for, as the trip left her dry and coughing with a throat full of dust.

The elderly man was Arman's father, who asked Sue to describe what had happened to their son. Sue explained the event and that it took everyone by surprise. She could not stop herself from crying as she explained the events that had transpired. After about ten minutes, she composed herself and respond to questions that were posed to her.

Arman's father advised Sue that the region was a dust bowl before Arman became an apostle. Once he was blessed, the total area prospered and converted to christianity. His brother studied theology and had become a priest and was asked to attend to Arman's funeral at their local church.

Arman told his parents that Sue had also become an apostle, and they advised Sue that they hoped she would stay in the region instead of returning to the Monastery.

Sue declined, as the Monastery was where she knew and had all the facilities she was accustomed to. She also had to attend to church services, as she was the only one there who could do the duties. They sat chatting for a while and then allowed Sue to go to her room to freshen up.

The room given to her was large and well furnished, with a very large bed and an area where Sue could sit at a table and do her work if required.

Sue freshened up and then went to see the sights. She had an escort, and they knew where to take her so she could get a better understanding of the region. After a couple hours of sightseeing, she returned to the mansion and to prepare for dinner.'

The dinner was a lavish affair, with several guests being invited. It was a formal affair for dignitaries and the influential families in the area and Sue was glad when it was over, and she could retreat to her room to rest.

The next morning, Sue was taken to a large church where Arman's body was on display. Many of the families that knew him came to pay their respects and pray over his body.

When all could see the body; Arman's brother began the ceremony and after an hour of prays and blessings, the coffin was sealed, and the service ended for a private burial. Everyone gathered at the family's private cemetery. Prayers were said, and those who wanted could place a rose on the coffin in memory of Arman.

Sue, instead of picking up a rose, grabbed a hand full of soil and stood in line, waiting for her turn to say her last goodbye. His father and mother were in front of Sue, and they placed their rose on his coffin and moved on, leaving Sue the only one left. All set their eyes on her as she stood there with her head bowed.

Sue approached the coffin, her head bowed, and gently placed a handful of soil on top. She whispered, 'To soil you shall return...... Wait for me in heaven with the Lord, my love. I will join you soon...... May the Lord bless your soul. May you rest in peace ..... Your work has finished on this earth, but mine has just begun.'

Sue found it hard to remove her hand from Arman's coffin. Arman's father had just moved on, but was close enough to Sue to hear what she had whispered. He stopped and turned, looking at Sue.

Sue stood there with both hands-on Arman's coffin with the dirt in one hand and the other hand moving to stop her from crying. No matter how much she tried, Sue could not control her emotions and burst into tears, crying over Arman's coffin.

Arman's father took her by the shoulder and led her back to her seat while she was still crying.

Sue could not control her crying and was led away from the plot to allow her to pull herself together and take control of her emotions.

She returned just as Arman's coffin was lowered into a prepared grave, and then the service ended. Everyone returned to the mansion for a wake, and many spoke in pleasant terms of Arman.

Mid way through the wake, Sue went to her room and packed her things for the next day's long journey back to the Monastery. Without being noticed, she left the gathering and went to her room. She sat for a while trying to understand why Arman had to die but couldn't come up with a reason. She sat there remembering Mary's words; that she would someday be in charge of the establishment and take over from Mary. How true was her prediction? Now she was in charge of it all, including having ministerial duties.

The only thought that went through her mind was the Lord used Arman to protect the Monastery and spread His word until Sue was ready to take over. She was always meant to be the Lord's Apostle, as she had the training and influence to do the Lord's work.

Sue sat in her room for a while and noticed that it was dark outside. She switched on the television to watch the news. She sat there for a while thinking, not concentrating as to what was being broadcasted. With Mary, Arman and the children gone, she felt empty and alone. She wondered how she would fill her life without them. All those she loved and cared for were now gone, and she was alone.

As she sat in her room, there was a knock at the door. Sue got up and opened the door, staring at Arman's father and mother, who asked if they could come in. She moved aside, letting them in, and closed the door behind them.

Arman's father said, 'We know you were in love with our son and, given time, most probably would have married him. He had confided in us about this. We want you to understand we consider you our daughter now and as part of our family.'

With that, Sue gave them each a kiss and thanked them for their kind gesture. Arman's father mentioned his son would often talk about you and we knew you were someone special to him. We understand that when he was killed, something was taken from you. We do not know why, but you are now our daughter and should treat us as your family and not left in this world alone. You have God and us.'

Sue thanked them and advised them she would be returning to the Monastery early in the morning and therefore would not see them before she left. She would return as soon as she could and understood she was part of their family and always welcomed and did not have to wait for an invitation.

Arman's father made it clear that the men will remain with her and would protect her from any attempt to injure her. With that, they gave each other a further hug and kiss and Arma's father and mother left Sues room.

She went to bed early because tomorrow's trip would be physically and emotionally demanding. She felt at home in Arman's house and could visit his gravesite at any time, but she ultimately decided to leave because she needed to be with her own children, Sarah and Timothy.

Sue slept throughout the night and woke up at dawn. She showered and went to have breakfast. She was the only one up and sat by herself. Afterwards, she went and collected her bags and brought them downstairs for the men to pack into the vehicle.

Arman's father was still in bed and the men were eager to get going. To express her gratitude for their hospitality and for taking care of her, she wrote a message to Arma's parents. She advised that the men looking after her were eager to go and, under the circumstances, she could do nothing but to leave them a note.

She went outside and got into the second vehicle. Then the escorts got in and they all drove off. Everyone was glad to be heading home.

They had driven for about two hours when they noticed a tree had fallen across the road. The troops knew this was an ambush and stopped all the cars some distance from where the tree had fallen across the road.

Half of the men went forward on foot to see who was setting up the trap. Sure enough, they spotted six men with guns behind some trees. In front of them were four bodies, presumably of those they had killed and robbed. To the left were two motor vehicles with bullet holes in the side panels and with smashed windscreens. In the cars were several women which were facing the back seats. Presumably shot at close range. No witnesses seemed to be the motto these killers followed.

The soldier in command called for a mobile rocket launcher and the man guarding Sue carried one up to where the men were positioned. Three of the men were to move across the road once the fighting began to try to get the other group into a crossfire.

The man with the rocket launcher aimed it at where they assumed the largest concentration of the killers were. On command, he launched the rocket, which hit the group with pinpoint accuracy. He then reloaded and launched a second rocket, which blasted the position of the second group. The soldiers then went in and killed the remaining attackers. They went through their pockets to get some identification as to where they came from, but no one had any ID on them. They didn't have any official orders, suggesting they were a group of renegade tribes' people looking to rob and kill those they encountered.

Arman's men attached a rope to the tree and pulled it across the road, to make sure that other drivers were not exposed to the same risk they were. They then drove off to continue their journey home.

Everyone was on guard from then on, knowing that bandits were out there setting up traps to kill for money and possessions. Everyone was glad when they finally arrived home and could drive into the Monastery and park.

Sue took her bags to her room and unpacked and went to see what had happened while they were away. She was glad to hear nothing out of the ordinary had occurred and things ran on as usual.

Sue wanted to create a seminary to teach young priests about the bible and train them to become ministers. It was hoped that those who graduated from the course would return to their region and establish the christian faith there.

While Sue was away, Nicholas advertised for applicants who wanted to become ministers. One university in America agreed to send some of their teaching staff to the Monastery on a rotation basis to help train these ministers.

The course would require three years of full-time studies, including being placed in churches during the breaks when semesters were not running. Thirty applications had been received, of which twenty were genuine applicants. The others applied to see if they were suited to becoming ministers and didn't know what they wanted out of life.

The courses involved mainly face to face lecturing, with several sessions being carried out on zoom.

A special lecture hall was built with a church alongside it to facilitate their training. In this way, trainees could gain practical experience by observing funerals, weddings, and other ministry activities. Also, the trainees were expected to hold sermons in their last year of training or at least help to write sermons as they showed their knowledge of the bible.

Sue was to be active in passing on her knowledge of the bible to the junior ministers, as she oversaw the school and the training of the ministers.

The visiting lecturers from universities would stay for a semester and then go back home after exams. Arman's men would protect the lecturers as they stayed in the Monastery. The school gained a reputation for training ministers for real-world scenarios instead of just focusing on academics.

Despite her busy lecture schedule, Sue would travel to both the States and Europe to speak about important social issues such as same-sex marriages, abortion, and euthanasia. She also was called upon to officiate at weddings, especially where those being married were film stars. She gained a reputation over the years for her forthrightness and honesty in her approach to sensitive topics.

CHAPTER 36

Sue was invited to speak at Cambridge University, England, where many speakers have made their mark, such as Spurgeon. She was excited about the offer until she saw the topic they wanted her to speak about: 'Are churchgoers honest or hypocritical about tending church?'

She thought about it and decided to take up the offer as England was a country where christianity and attendances at church were dwindling.

Sue arranged for the administration of matters at the Monastery in her absence and booked her flight to England. She left the Monastery in full sunlight on a warm and humid day and arrived finally in England where it was cold, raining and blowing a gale. Once she got out of the terminal, it was a fight to stay upright as she maneuvered to the taxi stand with her trolly full of bags.

There would be two speakers at the presentation. One for the proposition and the other opposing it. The arguments presented would be publicised in the university's journal, so a paper had to be submitted after the event.

Sue turned up on the day and was to be the second speaker. Statistical data from the first speaker's presentation suggests that young people no longer attend church solely to express their devotion to Christ. The Muslim population, who were growing through immigration, were the only ones who believed in a God, namely Allah. They were on track to outnumber the Anglo-Saxon population in England, within a decade.

The first speaker said, 'There are more people attending church in China than in England. Many young people in England no longer believe in Christ, the Bible, or the Holy Spirit. They see it as an ancient story that has lost its relevance in the modern age.'

The speaker said, 'This trend will continue, and elected leaders would provide benefits that the people wanted, and which were denied in the bible. People desire a decision-making approach that is more open-minded, allowing the government to decide rather than strictly following biblical restrictions.'

'The powerful would use the Bible to serve their own interests, which would make it lose its credibility in the western world.'

'Most people live their lives without recognizing the existence of a supernatural being. The majority did not give praises to God or concern themselves with sin. Most have not approached God nor have prayed to Him.'

'To tell the population that there is a God is to leave them with a lie. Science still says we grew over time to what we are at present without the intervention of a God. To tell people there is a God is misrepresenting the truth and lying to the population.'

'Those who go to church do so not out of belief but for social reasons or in the belief they are required to do what their parents taught them to do.'

'There is no God.'

The speaker left the stage with applause.

Sue waited for the applause to subside, then came to the podium and spread her papers out.

She says, 'In England, fewer people are going to church, but other countries are seeing record crowds every Sunday attending church.'

'We often hear someone saying, 'O God, why have you allowed this to happen?' If there was a true God, he would have intervened and stopped whatever from happening.'

'They therefore know of God.'

'Most of the population believe in God. It is just that they do not want to be seen to be in the minority.'

'People feel disbelief because they don't understand why we're here on earth and that God won't interfere until he's ready.'

'Most would prefer to see God governing earth now, so when something happens that is drastic, they immediately say this proves there is no God. If one existed, he would have immediately punished the perpetrator rather than allow them to seem to have got off scot-free with their crime.'

'They do not understand that all will eventually pay for their sins. Jesus Christ died on the cross to forgive those who genuinely seek his forgiveness, so seek his forgiveness to avoid paying for your sins later in life and ending up in hell.'

'Most people do not know why we are on this earth and what is required of us while we are alive. Most ministers do not explain this, leaving their congregation to find out for themselves. Where would you go to do this? Your local church, of course.'

'Church attendees can be characterised in three ways:'

'Those that go because it helps their image

These are not true believers and to them it is important to make an appearance to ensure they are recognised or thought of as being christians. Generally, this kind of person lacks faith in Jesus Christ and often requests a sign before believing, which never happens. They are the first to raise criticism against religion, tell jokes about the bible, Christ or swear in His name.'

'Those who believe in Jesus Christ but are not prepared to have total faith in Him.

These individuals go to church regularly and have part faith in Jesus Christ. However, they only dedicate an hour each week to worship and then decide what is right or wrong or best for themselves, hoping for Jesus' support. Their belief is that they are the god, and Jesus plays a supporting role to their requirements. If he helps great, but if he doesn't, then nothing is lost. They either idealise themselves or their partners, and in many instances, have statues of Budda or some other idle in their home. The more idles, the better.'

'They believe in respecting and following all religions, without favouring Christianity over others. Jesus in their eyes is not greater than the other heads of these other religions such as buddha. He is equal at best.'

'Instead of letting their idles go to waste, they believe accumulating them brings good luck to both them and their household. In the main, they are following satin in believing their fortune comes from either their good luck, good decisions or good fortune. These people tend to have good homes, cars and good jobs, the material things of life. They do not believe it is necessary to accumulate riches in heaven. They do not believe life on earth is temporary nor life in heaven is forever.'

If they are wrong and have misjudged the situation, they believe they can negotiate or mediate a successful outcome to enter heaven. Getting the best of both worlds.'

These are the people who ignore the presence of Christ when they face difficult situations that only Jesus can assist them with. Some people believe that if there was a God, the trials or bad luck wouldn't have happened.

They don't understand the purpose of the trials and think they're being punished for their sins.'

'They are part of the group who tend to have a major incidence when all things seem to be positive and heading in the right direction. The incidence tends to be sole searching and is meant to show how much faith they have in Jesus Christ. Instead of asking for his help, they move further away from the Lord and become lost.'

By valuing the State's regulations above the teachings of the bible, they can participate in practices like abortions, same-sex marriages, euthanasia, and transgender rights.

They claim to be devout Christians, but their support for state legislation in areas traditionally guided by biblical principles creates a conflict between religion and government.

'They choose to let the State decide what is right and wrong, instead of following the Bible and support the State instead of supporting the Bible.'

'The last category is the true believer who has total faith in Christ.'

'This group prays to the Lord for help, and God is part of their everyday life. In terms of how they should run their lives, they leave it up to God and seek his guidance in everything they do and thank the Lord for his help and support. They attend church as often as possible and read their bible regularly.'

'This person is often tested by trials to show them how much they believe in Jesus Christ. Most times, they are not wealthy and look to heaven for their reward. They seek eternal life as part of this.'

'Only a few people who go to church are true believers, and many of them face intense trials that cause them to lose their faith instead of strengthening it.'

'It takes time to find a true believer, and they often face multiple challenges that bring them to a low point in their lives. They get back on their feet eventually, but only after experiencing difficult times, which could mean the loss of a loved one or a financial trauma.'

'The true believer reads his bible frequently and follows the teachings of the bible rather than make up their version to suit the occasion.'

'Being a Christian means more than just an existence; it means a lifelong commitment to expressing your faith in Jesus Christ. Regardless of what happens, you maintain your faith by praying to the Lord for guidance and strength. To believe in Jessus Christ takes time to develop your faith and a lot of soul searching when trials bring you low and you ask the inevitable question, 'Why Lord? Why?'

'To be a christian is not to hide under a bush or run with the hounds. In many cases, it could force you to leave your friends and employment, as these places have showed they do not hold the same beliefs you do. Your friends, workplace, or family's negative attitude might lead you to either embrace your faith or reject Christ.'

'Those who attend church do so freely and with different purposes, as already explained. It is not up to the church to persuade the church goer to have faith in Jessus Christ. The church introduces people to Christ, and then Jesus takes over, strengthening their faith and bringing them closer to Him. This cannot be done by the church or the minister. Only Jessus Christ can reach out to you, and it is up to you to decide whether you will accept Him and follow his teachings or turn your back on Him and accept Satin.'

With that, Sue collected her papers and went back to her seat. There was no applause.

The co-ordinator stepped forward and thanked everyone for attending. Thanked the speakers and declared the meeting closed.

Everyone gathered and talked about the arguments for fifteen minutes. Afterward, Sue went back to her hotel for some rest because she had to make another presentation the next day.

CHAPTER 37

Sue realised the church could not wait for three years before the junior ministers were trained sufficiently to take over. She advertised to see if she could attract some qualified ministers to join the Monastery for a few years, or indefinitely. Even though she didn't expect receiving any applicants, she still placed an ad in several Christian journals and newspapers to test the waters.

James Jnr. was home one evening when his father collapsed, holding his chest, complaining of not being able to breathe. James called 911 and his father was rushed to the hospital with an expected heart attack. The roads were congested that day, and the ambulance could not get through without delay, resulting in his father dying in the ambulance.

James was all alone again and felt no one cared about him. He was a junior minister in a large church with little prospects for early promotion. He wondered what to do with himself. Everyone he spoke to suggested missionary work or move to another venue where the job prospect was better. James didn't want to move from home but agreed that a change in his geographics might be what was required.

One day on the subway, James found a newspaper and saw an advertisement for a minister willing to join a monastery for a year. He first did not entertain the thought, then decided to apply and see where he ended up.

Thinking nothing would come from it, he completed his resume and sent off his application. He received an acknowledgement and then a few days later, a letter advising his application had been received and was being considered.

A month later, he received a letter asking him to attend a formal interview at a hotel in his town. He attended as requested and made an impression with the Sue who did the interview.

Chapter 38

Sue received five applications and made appointments to interview them all in the States. If she was satisfied as to their commitment, she would fly them to the Monastery so they can see what they were getting themselves into.

Sue flew to the States and arranged to interview the applicants.

The first applicant wanted to travel while still attending to ministry work. Sue considered he would be more suited to missionary work and encouraged him to seek a year in Europe to get a different perspective on life.

The second applicant named Andrew, was an experienced minister and an academic. Sue was satisfied with his expertise, but believed he wasn't content with his current position. The only expectation his employer had of him was for him to conduct several masses a week, with no regard for the congregation or the content of his sermons. They cared more about the passing the plate around and collecting the takings than christianity. Sue invited Andrew to the Monastery, and wondered if he would get in trouble with his employer for seeking a new position. It was agreed he would seek annual leave and go to the Monastery during this period. If he was accepted, he would be required to teach junior ministers, research controversial Bible topics, and publish papers in religious journals. He was thrilled with these arrangements and was keen to visit the Monastery.

The third applicant, David, came from a large church and considered himself well trained and looking for a challenge. In his current environment, he was expected to go through the motions of holding mass and was given a roster when he was expected to do his part. Nothing was expected further of him. He would prefer to join a smaller setup where he could get to know the congregation and help them in their lives.

James, the fourth applicant, was well-trained in all aspects of ministry work. He was looking for a more challenging role than being one of twenty ministers. He would prefer to be with a smaller group and wanted to get more life experience than what he could get in his current position. His name was James and Sue was fascinated by him and wondered where she had met him before. He too agreed to join Sue on her return to the Monastery and planned to take a week off to fly there. Sue seemed to feel she knew James from somewhere but could not put her finger on it. Having received thorough training and possessing impressive credentials, he was well-prepared. He was the only child, and both of his parents had died, leaving him alone. He was single and had no family to worry about. Sue was keen to get him over to the Monastery, as she thought he would fit in well with how they ran things there. Arrangements were made for him to fly back with Sue and stay a few days.

The fifth applicant was not chosen because their preference was to work in a larger organisation with fewer daily challenges and less pressure to consistently perform well. He was happy to do his work and nothing further.

After the interviews, Sue booked her flight back home and arranged for the other three applicants to join her. She extended her stay by four days to attend lectures, allowing applicants to coordinate time off with their employers.

Everyone met at the airport and joined Sue on her flight back to the Monastery. When they landed they were met by Nicholas at the airport, who drove everyone back to the Monastery. Once there, all got out of the car and stood looking at the substantial building and the size of the establishment. Sue then escorted everyone inside and arranged for each person to have their own room. It was agreed that everyone would have an hour to freshen up and they would meet outside Sues's office to be given a guided tour of the establishment.

One hour later, everyone assembled, and Sue began the tour, introducing each person to the staff as they came across the main areas of expertise. Sue begun walking down the large hall to the orphanage. As she was moving along, she noticed James walking ahead of everyone as if he was trying to find something or knew where he was going. They stopped at an intersection and James yells out, 'The orphanage is just down this hallway and to the left!'

Sue wondered how he would know if he had never been here before. He walked into the orphanage as if he knew where it was. He also knew where the clinic was, which surprised Sue. The other ministers were impressed with the establishment and the school where junior ministers were being trained in small groups. They were told that they would need to share their expertise with junior ministers and help congregational members seeking spiritual guidance. This was what most of them wanted and it seemed all were keen to join the Monastery and hoped Sue would select them. Next was the visit to the church, and James led the way as if he knew where it was. When they entered the church, they stopped to have a good look at what was there. They all agreed it was the right size and would allow personal services to be handled. At the pulpit, they all expressed their desire to hold services and meet the congregation, something that wasn't possible at the larger churches they came from.

On their way to the clinic, they were amazed by the large hospital and nearby buildings where the doctors and nurses lived. They were taken to the outer perimeter and saw the military there, ready to stop any attack. The chances of an attack seemed lower now that the Monastery had grown. However, they were warned that an attach may occur at any time, and they should always be on guard as this was still deemed a hostile region. After the royal tour, all were taken to the dining room to have their dinner and to meet the staff. The children had been bathed and fed and could play before being put to bed.

Sue introduced the three applicants to those present and allowed them all to sit down to a meal which was basic but of good food. After they would ask questions and anyone present could give an answer in reply. The same was allowed of the staff and they asked each applicant a lot of questions, especially about their upbringing and expertise. Andrew saw the Monastery as the ideal place to advance his academic career without neglecting his ministry duties.

James surprised some of those present, as he could nominate Rachel and several other sisters before he was introduced to them. This surprised Sue, who put it down to hearing the names of the sisters and matching them up with persons who he came across. However, some sisters didn't think this was the case and thought something was strange about him. After the meeting broke up, it was agreed that they would adjourn to their rooms and get an early night's sleep. The applicants were glad to get into bed and rest up as it had been a full-on day, and most were tired from the long flight and the tour.

Sue couldn't stop thinking about James and the fact he seemed to know where the orphanage and clinic were in the complex. She thought about it and decided not to worry about it and went to bed.

The next morning, everyone was awakened at five in the morning and were ushered to the church for a service and prays. Afterwards, they could shower and have breakfast.

Sue decided to speak to James as to how he knew where the facilities were located. While the other applicants were at church, she brought James into her office and asked how he knew about the facilities and staff member's names.

James says, 'It seems as if you don't know me, Sue. I would expect the years to have changed me to some degree, but you of all people should still be able to recognise me.'

Sue was taken aback by this comment and just stared at James.

Sue says, 'No, I don't remember you yet at the interview I thought you looked like someone I loved in the past but convinced myself it couldn't be so.'

James says, 'The picture of you and Mary on your desk came home to me that this was the place I had been looking for, for years. I could never forget Mary as I was always with mum.'

Sue says, 'But how did you recognise Mary? She has never been with you, or has she?'

James says, 'It came back to me when we got out of the car, and I saw the Monastery and I then knew I found home.'

Sue says, 'Home you have never been here, and I doubt you would have met Mary in the States.'

James says, 'Sue, look at me. Who do you think I am?'

Sue looked at James for a moment and then shook her head in bewilderment and says, 'James, I am sorry, but I cannot place you. The first time I saw you was at the interview in the States.'

James says, 'I was an orphan here and let out for adoption. I was adopted by a minister at a large church in the States. After a year, he changed my name, and it was agreed to give me his name and to make my name my second name. I took his name and grew up as a normal American kid. My middle name is Rodney, 'Mum'. I was the kid always around you and Mary until I was adopted out. I could never forget this place as I was here for several years.'

Sue got up and said, 'Rodney the boy that I thought of adopting who would always be around me and call me mum after Mary died.'

Rodney said, "Yes mum.'

Sue burst into tears and stood up and hugged James. At that time, Sister Rachel was passing by Sue's office, heard her crying and entered her office.

Rachel says, 'Sorry, I could hear you crying. Is anything wrong?'

Sue, still sobbing, says, 'Do you recognise who James is?'

Rachel says, 'No, but I thought it strange for him to name me before you told him my name.'

Sue says, 'Rachel, this is Rodney, the little boy we sent to the States for adoption many years ago.'

Rachel looked at Rodney and then said, 'Yes, I believe it is him. I always remembered his smile and eyes.' She leaned over and gave him a kiss and a bug and said, Welcome home, Rodney.'

James says, 'When I was here, I remembered always playing with another friend, Tim, and his sister. Do you know what happened to them?'

Sue says, 'The boy was called Timothy, and his sister, Sarah. I attempted to adopt them, but the adoption manager was involved with a criminal gang. They ended up exploiting them for pornography or selling them off as sex slaves. We got the police onto them and after a couple of days, we found the manager of our orphanage in a gutter. He was shot dead, and the children were sexually assaulted and killed to ensure they could not name or identify those who were involved. Their bodies were burnt beyond recognition as a way of getting rid of them. Rachel and Arman were forced to identify them as best as they could. The bodies were buried in our private graveyard. We place flowers there just about every day. I can show you where they are buried if you are interested.'

James says, 'You seem upset at present. Maybe another day.'

Sue says, 'No, let's go and I will show you where they are.'

Sue got up and led the way, followed by James and Rachel. Upon arriving, James paused before the headstones, lowered his head, and offered a prayer for their souls to rest peacefully in heaven.

James asked a lot of questions about when, where, and why, but most of them couldn't be answered because the investigation never revealed the facts.

They all left after a while, with James being very tearful as to what had happened to the only friends he had at the orphanage. Everyone then went back into the main building, and each ended up shortly thereafter going to their rooms.

CHAPTER 39

Sue wanted to gauge the applicants' interest in joining the Monastery, so she invited them to her office the next morning to have a general discussion.

Everyone had a chance to share their thoughts and feelings about the positions and ask questions they had.

All three stated they were impressed with the facilities and were keen to accept the offer of employment for a minimum period of two years. They agreed to go back to the States and consider their future. When they're ready, they'll contact Sue to let her know if they'll accept the job offered. They would then have to give their current employer a formal notice of resignation and work out the period of their notice. The next morning, the new recruits packed their bags, said goodbye, and Nicholas drove them to the airport. They flew back to the States and returned to their normal routine.

They each took a week to think about it, and called Sue to confirm if selected, they would accept her offer of employment.

Sue initially wanted to fill only one position, but upon reflection, she decided to offer a position to each of the three applicants. She felt they would fit in and allow the establishment to grow and be recognised. It would also free up time for Sue to go to places and spread the Word.

She took their calls and was very happy that each agreed to join the Monastery and help grow what had been established.

Sue discussed the future with each applicant and offered them a job. They agreed on a start date that would give them enough time to give notice to their current employer. This applied to the other two applicants and not James. In his case, his employer was over staffed and was glad to dispense with the notice period, so he quickly made plans to fly back to the Monastery and start working immediately.

James went back to the Monastery and began assisting Nicholas and the sisters with conducting mass, funerals, and weddings. He fitted in well and made a good impression on all that worked with him.

After a month, James was joined by the other two applicants, and they created a schedule for assisting with church duties like holding mass and baptisms.

After two months, Sue felt sufficiently confident in accepting some appointments to lecture in the States. She would be required to take a week off to fly over there and to lecture or be a speaker at a rally or crusade. The ministerial work would be handled by those at the Monastery and not as previously forgone when she left to lecture. She also was called upon to attend to christian pilgrimages to other regions which had not been done since Arman's death. She was always escorted by Arman's men, who were fully armed, to take care of any attacks. They would not allow another person, insane or otherwise, to just walk up to Sue and shoot her as they did to Arman. This incident was never forgotten by them, and they never forgave themselves, allowing Arman to go to America without protection.

CHAPTER 40

Sue was determined to continue spreading the word of Jesus Christ, even though Arman died in tragic circumstances. She had planned on going north to Arman's region and then drive across to the adjoining region where the draught had taken hold. She originally wanted to travel alone, but she was persuaded to bring men with her because the area was still dangerous.

The convoy set off with two lead cars and the other vehicles driving in formation. It was a long ten hours to reach Arman's region and another two hours before they reached his father's house.

Sue was greeted as she disembarked from her vehicle and taken into the house. The men went to barracks that were allocated to them. Sue's bags were taken in and she unpacked, as she was going to stay for a few days. The region was prosperous and most of the population benefited from being of the christian faith.

She came because churchgoers informed her that certain ministers were imposing extra requirements on believers, such as giving a large portion of their income to the church and fulfilling other obligations. Ministers were encouraged to accept these additional requirements because it helped both the church and the wealthy individuals who donated part of their income.

Sue was asked to clarify the situation, as many patrons were prepared to lose their faith if this was true. She agreed to attend one of the large churches in the region and to give her sermon on this matter.

Sue went to the church on Sunday and fulfilled her role in the service. She then delivered a televised sermon from the pulpit, which was broadcasted throughout the region. Sue mentioned that many people have complained about the church adding extra requirements to become a good Christian. 'What you have been told is wrong and is designed to get you to either give the church more of your earnings or do other things such as being circumcised.'

'To be a good christian you only must believe in Jesus Christ. Nothing more. You must have faith in Jesus. Not yourself and think he is going to follow you as you make your decisions. If you want to make your own mind up and not seek God's help, then you can do as you please. Do not consider yourself a good christian when you give Christ one hour of your time on Sunday and the rest of the time you live your life according to how you wish. A good christian does not have to do additional things or perform additional rituals. All that a good christian must do is have faith in Jesus Christ. Let him organise and control your life. That is the sign of a good christian. What the church wants from you just increases the wealth of the church and has nothing to do with your faith in Christ. It is corrupt men trying to profit from religion. These men do not have Christ in their hearts but are persuaded by the devil. To follow them would eventually lead to your departure from the Christian faith and cessation of belief in Christ. Do not listen to them as they are not of this faith.'

Sue then stepped down from the pulpit. As she took her last step, one minister standing next to the pulpit tried to lunge at her with a knife in his hand, which hit the bible she was holding up.

One of Sue's security guards jumped up onto the stage and confronted the minister, who tried to stab the guard. He hit the minister with his fist, sending him flying. The minister then got up and tried to make a run for it but was held by other security men who came as soon as Sue was attacked. Sue was taken into an office next to the church until things settled down. After about fifteen minutes, she was allowed out of the office. Some patrons remained at the church, but the majority left, not wanting to witness how the church handled what Sue had said about their ministers.

In discussions with Arman's father, it was agreed that some of the qualified ministers from the school at the Monastery who had graduated would be placed at this church and other churches in the region to ensure they were acting in good faith. Those businessmen who tried to entice ministers from following the faith would be prosecuted and sentenced where a case could be brought against them. It was agreed that Sue should leave the region, as there was still the possibility that she would be in danger. It was agreed she would move onto the other region she planned on visiting, which was still subject to draught.

The next morning, Sue and her escort set off to see the other region that had been visited some time ago by Arman and Sue. The people turned from God and followed the State in matters that were contrary to the Bible, such as same sex marriage and euthanasia. They did not want to follow the teachings of the bible but follow the State's interpretation and so they formed over time a new belief and the State was God. Because of this, the Lord turned his face from them, and they were subjected to a server draught which has so far lasted five years. Many had perished from starvation, and most had lost their animals as there was no feed for them.

As they drove from the lush areas of Arman's father's region into the desert areas, they noted the lack of animals and people along the way. The area became arid quickly where it seems nothing could grow as there was no water. They drove for about two hours and could see only dust and carcases along the way. They finally came to a township and stopped to see if anyone lived there. After going through most of the shops there, it was apparent that no one was there. All had either left or died.

They got back into their cars and drove west for a further two hours and came across what seemed to be a reasonably modern house with a large barn at the back. They went up to the front door and knocked but received no answer. Entering the house, they walked through it to check if anyone was there. They found a pile of human bones in two of the bedrooms, showing that the occupants must have died from starvation some months ago. They went to the barn and found animal bones lying in some stalls, showing the animals had starved or were shot and left to die there.

It was agreed that they could do nothing to ease the situation, so they moved on and would camp in the open or at another place along the way. They drove off. An hour later, they stopped at a tree that was dead, but the main branches had not broken off.

Hanging from the main branch was a rope and under the rope piled on the ground was a heap of what seemed to be human bones. Someone could not bear the draught any longer and hung themselves. They left the bones and the rope and drove off, witnessing the severity of the draught. They drove another hour west and came across another farmhouse with a barn at the back. Again, they entered the premises and found remnants of the occupants who had died some time ago, possibly from starvation. The barn had no feed in it but had a tractor, and tools hanging from the back wall showing the prosperity of those who lived there. After looking around, they camped there for the night and drove the trucks into the barn and closed the doors. Everyone got out there cooking utensils and portable burners, and Sue and some men prepared the meal for the night. There was enough food for everyone and after washing the dishes, most went to sleep in their sleeping bags. The next morning, all had a light breakfast and after packing up, they resumed their journey.

After driving for three more hours, they stumbled upon a town that appeared to be in better condition than the towns they had seen the day before. They parked their cars at the beginning of the town and Sue and some men went to see if anyone was around. They walked through most of the establishments there without finding a soul and then drove through the town to see if the noise would bring someone out. Again, nothing. They decided to finish their journey by driving to the other side of the region and then would head back to the Monastery.

Two hours later, they began encountering areas with grass, showing they had left the drought-stricken areas and were approaching regions with some rainfall. After driving for an additional hour, they stumbled upon a small town where several individuals were gathered. They could see a church and headed for it first to see if anyone was around. They parked their cars and walked into the church and were greeted by a minister and two patrons who were surprised to see them, as it was rare for anyone to come there.

The minister told them that a handful of believers were able to settle here and survived by the grace of God. Water was provided from a rocky outcrop and food was reasonably plentiful from a few animals that they could graze. They knew of many who died in the drought and were waiting for it to pass so they could resume their lives.

After spending a few hours there, they embarked on their long journey home. They drove nonstop through the desert, only stopping when necessary, and finally reached the Monastery around midnight, relieved to be back.

Sue got up the next morning and had a pray session thanking the Lord for their safe return home.

CHAPTER 41

Sue had accepted an invitation to speak at several gatherings. The last of these was at Harvard University in Boston. She had left the Monastery a week ago and was looking forward to returning so she could take some time off and rest.

James and Andrew came along with her to see what it's like to speak at a rally in a big auditorium with a seating capacity of around twenty thousand students or more.

Andrew always wanted to preach the word to such an audience but was always held back because of inexperience and fear. James also found it intimidating to confront such a large gathering and was glad it was Sue and not him that was going to do the presentation.

Two speakers were to present. One for the proposition, the other against. The topic was "Was there really a Jesus Christ or is he a figment of our imagination?"

There was to be two speakers. The first was well known in his field and was known to be an atheist who was to argue against the proposition. Sue was the second speaker, arguing for the proposal.

The academic started off first and asked the crowd has anyone had ever seen Jesus Christ. No one answered. He then asked, 'Does anyone believe he exists? The answer was a clear no. He then asked if anyone had ever witnessed a miracle. Upon hearing another negative response, he sat down, already expecting Sue's input to be disregarded.

Sue stood up and moved to the podium. She spread her papers and adjusted the microphone. She then spoke. Unfortunately, no one could hear her speak because of the noise the placard crowd would not shut up and kept getting louder and louder. At what seemed to be the loudest point, a man jumped up on the stage and moved towards Sue. James and Andrew stood up as they were on stage, with Sue fearing there was going to be trouble.

Approaching Sue where she was standing, the man says to her, 'Let me speak to them.'

Sue moved to the side, and the man moved in front of the microphones. He had a compact unit on his belt, which he took off and moved it to the microphones and pressed the top. With a loud, ear-piercing noise omitted, everyone stopped speaking and quiet fell upon the crowd. He moved to the microphone and said my name is Barabbas and I have come to hear the speakers, not you lot of placards carrying idiots. Shut up or if you want to speak, get out and let those of us who want to hear the other side do so.

The crowd started raising its voices, 'Crucify him.' He then let out another screech from his unit, which then stopped the noise and again quiet fell upon the gathering.

He said to Sue, you can resume and motioned her to commence speaking. Sue was in the proses of thanking him when she could see he didn't understand her. He then took out the earplugs out of his ears and says, 'You're welcome' and stepped off the stage and resumed his seat.

Sue said, 'It is obvious that most of you do not know Jesus Christ nor have time for him. If you keep going this way, you'll eventually feel the need to explain why you didn't listen to him while you were alive. Once you're gone, it'll be too late. He will say, 'You didn't want to know me on earth, then be gone with you to hell, for I do not know you in heaven.'

In summary, Jesus Christ is the son of God, the creator of heaven and earth. He was borne of the virgin Mary and became man, crucified for our sins and was buried. He rose on the third day and finally was resurrected and now sits on the right hand of God in heaven. The key is to have faith in Jesus Christ, who died for our sins. If you believe in Him, He takes away your sins and gives you the chance for an eternal life with God in heaven.

Extensively, he preached as a man on this earth. He did show signs, but no one was prepared to acknowledge them. He raised lazaret from the dead and made many who were crippled walk again. Despite making the blind see, these miracles went unnoticed or were noticed, but people refused to acknowledge them.

You get up every morning and see the sunrise and a new dawn, yet you say, 'Show me a sign'. You see, the rainfall and the grass grow along with flowers and yet you still want a sign. And you stand around with placards to stop free speech. Why don't you live in Russia or China where they have already done what you desire? There is no free speech there. You speak out and you're dead or in prison. They are the countries you should pack your bags and go to, and they will facilitate your desires. No, you stand protesting and stopping free speech here but would not go where they have already done what you are trying to achieve in America.

There are things on this earth that you don't see but know are there such as sunlight, the wind, earthquakes, yet you know they are present. Yet you refuse to acknowledge the Holy Spirit being present and refuse to acknowledge Jesus Christ as king. Why? Because you believe in yourself as God and refuse to acknowledge the true God.

There is a God who created you and who loves you. Stop messing around with this placard waving garbage and get to know the true God before it is too late.

The crowd gathered on Palm Sunday to praise the Lord as he entered Jerusalem three thousand years ago.

One week later, the same man stood before Pilot.

'Pilot said I have this criminal who has killed without concern and has even killed your own kinfolks.'

'Who of these two would you want me to set free? The man known as Jesus or the criminal Barabbas.'

Pontius Pilot says, 'And what would you have me do with this man, Jesus?'

The crowd yells back, 'Crucify him!'

They yelled loader and loader, making sure any opposition could not be heard.

The Lawmakers yelled out. 'Crucify him.'

The today's managers yell out, 'Crucify him.'

Today's workers yell out, 'Crucify him.'

Today's youth yell out, 'Crucify him.'

Today most of the population yell out, 'Crucify him.'

Today's religious academics yell out, 'Crucify him.'

Today, most religious ministers of churches yell out, 'Crucify him.'

Then Pilot says, 'I wash my hands of this matter. Let it be upon your soul as to what you do with him.'

HE WAS CRUCIFIED. DEAD AND BURIED.

And on the third day rose and appeared before many who witnessed and verified it was He.

He was resurrected on the third day and now sits on the right hand of God in heaven.

'Do you believe this?'

I fear not, for the truth has been buried and most of you do not read the bible to decide what is true but change historical events to suit your own agenda. If you don't want to follow the way of the Lord, you will find excuses as to why you must do something instead of following his word.

Jesus, in one of his parables, said. 'A rich man invited all to come to his banquet. No one came. All made excuses. I have a horse to take care of, or I must dig a well. And so it is now. But when the day of reckoning comes, it will be too late for you.

Wave your placards and yell out, 'Crucify Him', for he knows who you are and what you have become. A mad rabble manipulated by the powerful to ensure they rule your lives and not Jesus. Be a puppet for them and one day you will wake up, but it will be too late. Just think who gave you the placards and who is paying you to demonstrate and ensure I do not get a say at this university. Isn't this denying a person their democratic right to speak? What you are trying to do is to stop me from presenting what the Bible has to say. Continue along this path and one day this will be done to you and your children. When you stop following the bible and listen to the rich and powerful who run this State. They want you to give up your God and accept them in place of Jesus Christ.

Sue then went back to her seat, and after the MC closed the debate, walked off the stage, thanked the chairman for his support and kindness, and walked out with James and Andrew to where her car was parked and went back to her hotel. They went to the Bistro, and each ordered a meal. Once they had eaten this, they went to their rooms to rest.

The next morning, Sue, Andrew, and James met at the restaurant for breakfast before heading to the airport. However, just as they were about to leave, Sue got a call from Barabbas asking for ten minutes of her time. She pointed out they were in a hurry to catch a flight back to the Monastery and time did not permit her to meet with him. He said he would meet her at the airport and talk to her as she booked in.

Sue arrived at the airport on time and walked in just to be met by Barabbas. She grabbed her luggage and walked over to book them in, followed by James and Andrew. All went to check in and once they booked themselves in and their luggage, Sue sat down with Barabbas to see what he wanted.

Barrabas wanted a job and began talking to Sue about a special service for teenagers and those in their early twenties. He reckoned that the traditional service puts this group off, and he could rejuvenate this group. Sue could see what he wanted to achieve and said she would want to see the mass as he envisaged it to be conducted before allowing him to proceed. One thing she did mention was that he continually referred to the use of music as part of the mass. To achieve this, you would need a band. Sue asked him about this, and he revealed he was a musician before he became a minister and could play a variety of instruments and the piano. He had three other musicians which made up his band, and each was an accomplished musician.

Sue was still doubtful about Barabbas, as his appearance was not conventual. He had tattoos all over his arms and some on his face. He had a steel ring on his nose and wore earrings in both ears. Furthermore, there was a ring on one of his eyebrows, and Sue could understand how that could be comfortable. Yet he could prove he completed his studies in religion and was a minister of religion. Wherever he went, they rejected him because of his appearance and rejected the idea of having a special mass for the youthful with music and preaching. No one wanted to adopt his concept and told him to get rid of the steel nose ring and tattoos, otherwise he could never get a job and not preach the word. Their theory was if you want to preach about the Devine and saints then you should look like one.

At that point of time, Sue received the message over the loudspeakers that her flight was boarding and, therefore, had to say goodbye to Barabbas. It was agreed he would ring her later during the week, when they could discuss the matter further.

When she got back to the Monastery, Sue immersed herself in her work, which had piled up while she was away in the States. Barrabas called her during the week, and they agreed to meet in two weeks in Boston to discuss their plans. Sue was due to speak at a rally there, and it would be an excellent opportunity for Barabbas to show her what he could do to excite the younger crowd.

Two weeks came around quickly, and Sue again found herself in the States with James to assist her and to get experience as to how to preach to a large audience.

Barabbas and his band were scheduled to meet Sue at the venue. They agreed to perform music during two sessions, which Barabbas would also preach at. Rehearsal was to begin immediately, even though all the speakers were not present.

Sue began the rally, followed by Barabbas, who sang two hymns. Then, another speaker would come up, and finally, Barabbas would give a lecture with his band backing him up.

It was apparent from the start that Barabbas and his band hit the right keys. As soon as they played, everyone stopped to listen, and it was not long before the word got around, and everyone wanted to come and hear them. Rehearsal went well and everyone present knew when they were expected and the frequency. It wasn't long before the day arrived and the crowd assembled, filling the large hall to capacity.

The first speaker stepped up to the podium and thanked everyone for coming and introduced the speakers to the crowd. They all then went offstage, leaving the first speaker, who spoke about God's love for everyone. He then was followed by Barabas and his band, who excited the crowd, receiving a long and loud applause after they completed. Barabas then spoke, and he was followed by his band with more music. Sue then spoke, and she was to some extent followed by background music from Barabas's band. There was an eerie quietness thru out the stadium, which housed fifteen thousand people. All listened intensely to what Sue had to say, and it seemed her message got thru. She was followed by another speaker and then Barabbas and his band, and so on.

Everyone agreed that the evening went well, thanks to Barabbas and his band, who broke up the monotony of the speakers.

After that evening, calls came in for Barabbas and his band to take up gigs all over the country and they became booked up, months in advance. Barabbas not only got recognition for his band, but also became a lecturer and preacher. He even secured a permanent position at a large church that aimed to engage more young people. He was grateful for Sue's help and would sometimes bring his band to perform for the sisters and the appreciative crowd outside the Monastery. It was not long before Barabbas and his band were earning more than the average circuit speaker. However, as they got older, they would lose some of their following even after introducing new songs.

To keep 'Cool' and in with the young followers, Barabbas would have to reinvent himself or as the bible puts it 'He would have to be born again'. No doubt wisdom will prevail and he will do this as time goes by to ensure he is useful to the Lord in spreading the word to the younger generation.

CHAPTER 42

Many years had passed and Sue, over time, had gained a reputation for fighting for the Christian faith. At first, she would step back and let those involved in the church or academics take the lead, but this rarely happened because many of them didn't believe in Jesus Christ. They were there to make a living, not to believe or have faith in Christ.

Sue would appear on television and radio to answer the criticism or outright lies and to put the christian perspective forward.

It was in the afternoon, and Sue was finishing writing up one of her sermons in her office. She needed some air and went to the garden at the back of the buildings to cut some flowers to place on Sarah's and Timothy's grave.

As she walked down the long hall, she could see a woman standing there to the left and thought she was lost, or she was looking for the medical centre or the orphanage.

Sue walked up to the women and said, 'Can I help you? You seem to be lost'.

The women stopped, turned to stare at Sue and said nothing for a moment or two, then said, 'Sue, don't you remember me?' She paused and then said, 'I'm Sarah.'

Everything went blank in Sue's mind, and she immediately fainted, falling limb to the floor.

Sarah immediately rushed over to her and turned her over and reached into her pocket for a bottle of smelling salts. She also had a two-way radio with her so she could be reached. She reached for it and called for help. Within minutes, two men arrived and loaded Sue onto the stretcher, which they brought with them. They took Sue to award and put her in a bed. Sarah immediately hooked Sue up to a monitor to read her blood pressure and oxygen level. It showed her blood pressure was low and so was her oxygen level. Sarah reached for an oxygen mask and placed it over Sue's mouth. As the levels came up, so did her blood pressure. Sarah again placed some smelling salts under Sues nose, which brought Sue around. She was groggy at first, then appeared normal staring at Sarah.

After a few minutes, Sue says, 'Sorry I alarmed you. When you said your name was Sarah, I thought you were someone else, but I now realise you're a different Sarah. What a co-incidence that you have the same name as a child I once tried to adopt.'

Sarah said, 'That is exactly what I am saying. This man standing near me is Timothy, the boy you wanted to adopt, and I am Sarah, the one who you placed at the bottom of the cross and the Lord in His mercy fixed my paralysis.'

Sue says, 'No. This can't be. My Sarah was executed by drug barons, and we found her body along with Tims in a burnt-out house. We barely recognised them, and they are interned in our private graveyard at the back of this building. I place flowers on their graves each day. So, you must be another Sarah.'

Sue stared at both, not believing Sarah. She looked at Timothy and could see the boy in the man, but this could not be the case. Sue said, 'We received word from the police that the criminal element had raped you both and killed you to ensure you did not tell the police about their crimes. To ensure no one recognised the bodies, they burnt them, and we were asked to identify you.'

'I couldn't face looking at your mangled and burnt bodies. Arman and Sister Rachel weren't completely sure, but they thought it was probably you, since there was no other information about what happened to you.'

'We need to gather the sisters who were involved in identifying the burnt bodies. They should hear about your life after you left the orphanage. We will arrange it for this coming Sunday at two in the afternoon in the church hall.'

Tim then stepped forward and said, 'When you feel better, we can meet and tell you our story as to what had happened to us. For now, you should rest, and we will come back in about two hours' time and if you're alright, release you from the hospital so you can sleep in your own bed tonight.'

With that, Tim and Sarah left Sue and went back to their work. Sue laid back in the bed she was placed in and closed her eyes to rest.

Two hours later, Sarah comes back to check on Sue. Her blood pressure and oxygen levels were normal, and Sue could concentrate better as she had a brief nap and felt much better. Her mind was not all over the place and she could concentrate on what was being said and what she was saying.

Sue got out of bed and supported herself by the bedrail until she got her balance.

Sarah said, 'When would it be convenient for us to come and tell you our story?'

Sue says, 'Come tomorrow at ten in the morning and we will see what you have to say. I will invite other people to the meeting. People such as Rachel, who attended to you when you were in the orphanage and James, who you used to play with. They will be able to see if you are the Sarah who was in our orphanage. Do you remember a boy called Rodney?'

Sarah said, 'I remember Rodney and I am shore Timothy would too, as we always used to play together and all of us used to call you Mum.'

Sarah said, 'Good, we will be there and tell you our story. Now can you show us where we are buried so we can place some flowers on our graves.'

Sue got out of the bed and, in a wobbly fashion, took Sarah and Timothy to the gravesite where they buried the children, who they thought were Sarah and Timothy.

Sarah bowed her head and said a pray over the two graves. They stayed there for another fifteen minutes and then everyone separated to attend to their normal day's routine.

Sue and Sarah then walked slowly to Sue's room. Once there, Sarah made sure Sue could manage. The room appeared the same as when she last saw it, when Sue would take her there, to collect papers or for some privacy reasons.

Sarah then left Sue to go back to work. Sue called some nurses and sisters from the orphanage and invited them to a meeting tomorrow at two in the afternoon. They would get a chance to meet Sarah and Timothy and learn about their experiences with the man who wanted to adopt them. She told them about Sarah and Timothy and that they say they are the children who Sue was going to adopt.

Sue then telephoned James and told him what had happened. He was dumfounded as he never in his wildest dreams thought he would ever see Sarah and Timothy again. He would cut it close as he had a meeting with a couple that wanted to book in their wedding, but he was sure he would get there.

Everyone Sue contacted was eager to hear from the two doctors and find out what had happened to them. They told Sue that they thought the buried children were Sarah and Timothy. However, they agreed to come and see for themselves and decide if they were the same children they had cared for in the orphanage as they claim to be.

CHAPTER 43

The room selected had about thirty people waiting to see Sarah and Timothy and to hear what had happened to them. Both Sisters Adrian and Reilly were there as they were asked to identify the bodies of the children who were subsequently buried at the Monastery.

Sarah arrived first and Timothy shortly after. Nothing was said with everyone staring at them to see if they were the babies that were given to the orphanage. The Sisters had pictures of the babies and passed copies of these around to those who wanted a copy. A copy was also given to Sarah and Timothy.

Sue stepped up before the gathering and said, 'No doubt you all have gathered here to identify these two doctors who say they are Sarah and Timothy. I have already explained to them what had happened to Arman, as they both asked about him by name. Neither were prompted nor helped to name him. They spoke of him as they knew him well and both said they thought he was their father.'

'For their information, I will briefly advise what had happened from our end so we all can try to pull the pieces together. The doctors haven't been given your names, so they might have to remember them on their own. They remember all of you taking care of them when they were orphans here.'

Sue continued and said, 'I applied to adopt both of you, but was unsuccessful in doing so. The then manager who ran the department refused my application on the bases that they wanted you to go to a married couple who could not have children of their own.'

'I was told that a couple applied to have you adopted. They did police and character checks, and the adoption manager believed it was the best course of action for both of you to be adopted by them.'

'I refused to accept this and with Arman; we attempted to get your file to satisfy ourselves that this was the case. Our efforts were hindered by the adoption manager and his staff, who refused our request to see your file. Not being satisfied what was told to us, we used my master key to unlock the office and examine your file.'

'We found out that the adoption manager was connected to a criminal gang involved in pornography. They gave you to, two criminals as possible adoptees.'

Sue was in tears by now, but still pressed on.

Sue said, 'We alerted the FBI, who after a few days advised us they located the manager who had been shot in the head. They also advised they had located two bodies of children who fitted the description of the children taken from our orphanage. The bodies of the children were disfigured to the degree that the two sisters and Arman, who went to identify the children, could not recognise them. No identification was made but based on probability, it was considered that they were the two children we were looking for.'

Sarah burst into tears, and she went up to Sue and put her arms around her and said, 'You must have been devastated when you heard what the FBI said to you.'

Both wept and could not control their emotions.

The meeting was temporarily stopped to allow Sue and Sarah to regain their composure. Everyone gathered around Sue and Sarah to try to comfort the two. A glass of water was given to each of them, which they sipped from.

After about twenty minutes, they all resumed their seats and Sue continued.

Sue says, 'I could not go and identify the bodies, as I had completely lost it by then. Two of the sisters and Arman went to identify the bodies. As previously stated, no positive identification was made, but based on probability, it was concluded that the bodies were the two children who we were looking for.'

'We buried the children in the Monastery's cemetery and named them Sarah and Timothy, as we believed they were our two children. I tried to resume my career but ended up in a mental hospital and received shock treatment before being rescued by Arman and the sisters.'

Sue intentionally didn't nominate the two sisters who went to identify the bodies. She already told Sarah and Timothy about what happened to Arman and why he was not at the gathering.

Sue says, 'I will now pass the stage to Sarah and Timothy and allow everyone to hear from them.'

Sarah said, 'It is extremely upsetting to hear the story as told by Sue and no doubt you all suffered from that experience.'

To start, let me try to name a few of you whom we had dealings with in the past. Sue pointed to Sister Adrian and said we remember you as Adrian as you were always with us when Sue could not make it. You too were our mother after Sue.'

Sister Adrian said, 'I am glad you remember me and, like Sue, I to consider you as part of my family.'

Timothy then said, while pointing to a sister, 'You are Sister Reilly, as you were mostly with me, especially bathing me when Sue was away.'

Sister Reilly acknowledged he was right.

They both named two more sisters and nominated four others that were close to them and instances that had happened to them while in their care. The photos showed a likening to them, and it was not long before the group concluded they were the true Sarah and Timothy.

James came into the meeting ten minutes late and wasn't noticed by Sarah and Timothy. After everyone had their turn, he stood up and said, 'My name is James. Do you remember me?

Sarah and Timothy looked at James but couldn't place the name. Sarah said, 'No sorry I don't recall a James when we were here. We always played with Rodney, and you look a bit like him, but older.'

Timothy says, 'You are Rodney, you're not James.'

James says, 'It is a long story. I will fill you in later.'

The meeting concluded with everyone satisfied the two were Sarah and Timothy. James went down and met with his friends and went away with them to tell his story and to hear there's.

The meeting decided to take a break so that everyone could attend to their responsibilities. They planned to meet again the following day to hear Sarah and Timothy's account of what had happened to them.

Sue went back to work, but only sat there thinking of the three children and what will happen now. She was shortly joined by them, her family.

CHAPTER 44

Sue was sitting at her desk trying to complete paying some bills when Sarah and Timothy came in and stood at the door. Sue looked up and saw them there and stood up to greet them.

Sarah said, 'You still find it hard to accept that we are the children you intended to adopt, aren't you?'

Sue says, 'Yes, as I had come to terms with the fact that the ones we buried were the children I was going to adopt. It makes it hard with Arman not being here. I relied on him a lot and with you two out of my life and then Arman, I sometimes feel alone and have no one to turn to for comfort except God, who is always there. Thankfully.'

Sarah said, 'Can we ask what happened to you after you buried the children? We have heard whispers you became very ill and ended up in a mental hospital. Is that true?'

Sue says, 'Yes, I had a nervous breakdown shortly after we buried the children. I was on a set filming when I saw two children who looked like both of you. Despite what everyone was telling me, I would not accept that you were dead. Jesus was not someone I believed in at that time, only in myself. I thought I could overcome all things. I ended up in hospital and they tried a variety of drugs on me, but my mental state was deteriorating quickly, so they gave me shock treatment. They convinced Arman that this was the only way out and he agreed to it. The treatment left me without a memory. I knew no one and could not remember people or locations. I was getting worse when Arman collected me and brought me back to the Monastery. He placed me under the cross and the good Lord had mercy on me and brought me back to life. After that I become a voice for God and took up several invitations to preach the bible and to spread the word.'

'I became a disciple and would go with Arman to spread the word and when he died, I would go on my own, protected by the Holy Spirit.'

Sarah said, 'What happened to Arman?'

Sue says, 'His time had come as what was predicted by Sister Mary. She said I would run the Monastery. I never believed her. Me, a film star running a large complex like this one. I never thought that it would ever happen. Now I take trips around the world speaking for the Chistian Faith. While we were finishing a church service in a northern region, some men started shooting at us. They shot Arman, who was leading the service, directly in the heart. He died within seconds of being shot. I wept over him as he was the one I loved but could never have. Same happened with the children. I finally decided to adopt them, and they were taken from me.'

Sue began to weep, and Sarah got up and hugged her tightly and says, 'You certainly have had a hard time losing everyone that was close to you.'

Timothy moved up to her and says, 'We are here and will stay with you from now on.'

Sue kissed Timothy on the cheek, then returned to her chair to continue their conversation for another hour. She had to excuse herself afterward so she could complete what was necessary for tomorrow's meeting.

CHAPTER 45

Sue entered the hall and could see Sarah and Timothy sitting, waiting for others to arrive.

The room filled quickly and after fifteen minutes, Sue moved forward and said, 'Thank you for coming. We are here to hear two people tell their story as to what had happened to them after they were taken by the criminal gang. What we would also like to decide are these two doctors, our Sarah and Timothy, the children we knew and took care of in our orphanage. It has been twenty years, and those who knew Sarah and Timothy should try to confirm if they are the same orphans who were given up for adoption.

Sarah moved to the front of everyone and says, 'Thank you, Sue. Over the last two days, we have introduced ourselves to many of you whom we could name and had discussed events we remembered as children here. This has assured us that this is the place we used to know as home, and you are the people that looked after us. You were all our parents.'

'Now let me tell our story so we can fill in some of the gap between our adoption and now. Both of us will provide bits of information and we will try to keep it as simple as possible. There will be many facts that we just don't remember.'

Sarah handed the microphone to Timothy, who paused, looking at the crowd of people that came to hear their story.

Timothy said, 'I am older than Sarah and therefore most of the recollections were mine. We were awakened that morning and told that we were going to be adopted. I asked was Sue adopting us and told yes, but she was not here and was in America waiting for us. I was told she sent a man to take us to the States, and we were to hurry as we could not afford to miss the plane. We were dressed, and one lady from the office took us to the airport. While waiting for this man who was flying in to pick us up, we were given breakfast at the airport.'

'The man arrived after a long wait and spoke with the women who was taking care of us. She gave him some books, which no doubt were passports to allow us entry into the United States. He took us by the hand and led us to a lounge. Sarah could not walk the distance, so he had to carry her. Once at the lounge, he sat us in a seat and told us not to move. I got up and moved around as he was trying to validate our boarding pass. He came up to me and said, 'I told you to sit in your chair and not to go anywhere. He was angry when he found out I disobeyed him, and he slapped me. I cried, and people nearby wanted the police to come and arrest him for hurting a child.'

'The man became more aggressive, and the police were called, but he made a run for it, leaving all our things on the chair next to us. Since our boarding pass had been validated, an airline hostess took us on board and strapped us in our seats. The assumption was that someone would be waiting for us in America. What we didn't know was the hostess was also being paid by the mob to make sure we reached America. She looked after us during the flight, feeding us and giving us drinks. Eventually we arrived in America and were walked off the plane. We seemed to have walked miles and had to go through several checkpoints till finally we were handed over to a man who said we looked just like his children.'

'The man carried Sarah, and I was told to keep up with him. I am sure most of the time he was dragging me along as he walked very quickly, and I could not keep up with him. He finally got a luggage trolly and put us both in it and pushed it out of the airport to a waiting car.'

'We were transferred to the car, which sped off to a unit which we believe was in New York. We were held there for a couple of days. During this time, more children were brought in. Several of them were stripped naked and taken out to be filmed. Afterwards, some men took them, and we never saw them again. All that we could hear was them screaming, which lasted for a long time, and then everything went quiet. I saw one girl lying on the floor, motionless and naked in one room, which had a bed in it and nothing else. There is little doubt she was dead from the constant raping that was inflicted on her. She would have been six years old or thereabout.'

'After seeing this, I went back and took Sarah out of the room we were in and walked down a large hallway and got a lift to the ground floor. We then walked out of the building and down the street. We kept off the main roads and tried to walk along the street where there was little traffic. Unfortunately, we were spotted by the police who took us in their car. They were alerted by the gangsters to be on the lookout for us. While we sat in the car, we could hear them phoning them and they were going to take us back to the unit we came from.'

'The policeman stepped out of his car to buy us a drink. We could see him at the counter. So we opened the door of his car and ran to hide from him.'

'When he came back, he kept driving around to see if he could spot us until he gave up. We walked for miles and got some food from raiding restaurant's garbage tins. Eventually, we sought shelter on a veranda and spent the night there. We were awakened by women who found us there when she went to collect her mailbox. She took us into her home and fed us. After asking us a lot of questions, she phoned the FBI, who sent two men to question us. After listening to our story, they reported us to the department, who looked after fostering children. At their insistence, we were allowed to stay with the couple who found us.'

'A few days later, we heard on the news that some gangsters had been caught trafficking in pornography and selling young children as sex slaves. Some gangsters tried to shoot their way out of the siege and were killed. It was also noted that records left behind implicated some police in the area and showed an extensive network of those who were tied up with the mob.'

'The couple who found us on their veranda fostered us for several years, and then legally adopted us as their children. Both parents were doctors, and they were unable to have children, so it made their family complete with us being adopted. Both of us took an interest in medicine and they put us through medical school. They have since died and left their estate to us to be divided equally.'

'We've been searching for this place for the last ten years, going to many places around the world who needed doctors for humanitarian work. Having visited most of the African and South American countries, we noticed your advertisement for doctors. We subscribed for half a year as we had not been here before and didn't know what to expect. It was luck or an act of God that led us here. Now you know our story.'

The audience was shocked and angry to learn about the terrible treatment the two children received after being adopted by criminals. They were treated as a commodity which was sold for profit. No one cared what happened to them other than ensuring they survived to be sold to the highest bidder.

Timothy said, 'This practice still goes on today and pornography and slave trading are on the increase and have become big business, protected by the criminal mobsters.'

'Some agencies updated their adoption rules to avoid similar problems, while others stayed with the old rules, hoping fraudsters wouldn't try the same thing again. These organisations were fooling themselves and have made this decision because someone in their organisation is being paid to do so.'

The final census amongst the meeting was that they were the children adopted out and everyone was happy to see their return to the Monastery.

Sue had her family back again after each had been taken from her. What would they have been if they stayed with her and what would have happened to her after she no longer was accepted as a glamourous film star?

God had many things to straighten out.

Arman's background was tribal, and he became a forceful element in establishing christianity in the region. A lone minister would not have had the expertise to do this, as initially there was more combat than preaching. Through the years, he was moulded into this position. He was a leader, a fighter, and then became a preacher, an apostle.

Sue loved Arman and planned to marry him, but their glamorous lifestyles could have driven them apart, and possibly divorce. By the time they married, both would have been too old to adopt the children.

They both came from different backgrounds and initially looked for different things out of life. Sue a glamourous career in the spotlight, while Arman a leader of a tribe and then an apostle.

There is no doubt Sarah and Timothy would not have become doctors and James a minister of religion if they stayed with Sue. They no doubt would have been encouraged to enter the film industry. Many try, but few succeed, so we do not know what could have become of them. Many also end up on drugs and crash, so who knows?

Sue's acting experience helped her feel confident speaking at big events and presenting a compelling case for nonbelievers to consider Jesus' offerings.

The Bible tells us that all we can do is spread the word. The rest is up to the Lord to convert the person from a nonbeliever to a believer.

Rodney, Tim, and Sarah have been trained for their chosen occupations by God. They were then sent back to Sue as a family to live their lives together.

God tests all to show you how much faith you have in him. He did this to Job and he will test you. In Sue's case, she was made ill and had to enter a mental hospital. She lost everything and even tried suicide. No one could make her better. Only Jesus was able to do this.

God gave her health back to her and returned her children. Arman is in heaven waiting for them.